"Listen, Long," the sheriff said in a cold voice. "You've rode roughshod over me about as long as I'm gonna stand for it. Now, you get out of my office and you stay out of my office. You ain't welcome in this jail anymore and you ain't going to use it for your personal lockup. I don't care if you are a federal deputy marshal." He put his hand near the butt of his revolver. It was not quite a threatening gesture, but it had implications.

Without pause, Longarm drew his revolver and thumbed the hammer back. It made a loud *clitch-clatch* in the room. "Now, I'm only going to say this once, Sheriff. You either stay out of this, or I'm going to put you in one of those cells with these men. You are interfering with a federal officer in the performance of his duty and that is a felony, and I will damn well put you in jail and bring you to trial for it. Do you understand me?"

➤ **TABOR EVANS** ◄

LONGARM

AND THE
SAN ANGELO SHOWDOWN

J

JOVE BOOKS, NEW YORK

LONGARM AND THE SAN ANGELO SHOWDOWN

A Jove Book / published by arrangement with
the author

PRINTING HISTORY
Jove edition / January 1995

All rights reserved.
Copyright © 1995 by Jove Publications, Inc.
This book may not be reproduced in whole
or in part, by mimeograph or any other means,
without permission. For information address:
The Berkley Publishing Group, 200 Madison Avenue,
New York, New York 10016.

ISBN: 0-515-11528-2

A JOVE BOOK®
Jove Books are published by The Berkley Publishing Group,
200 Madison Avenue, New York, New York 10016.
JOVE and the "J" design are trademarks
belonging to Jove Publications, Inc.

PRINTED IN THE UNITED STATES OF AMERICA

10 9 8 7 6 5 4 3 2 1

LONGARM

AND THE
SAN ANGELO SHOWDOWN

Chapter 1

Billy Vail, United States Marshal, First District Court of Colorado, said, "The army is asking us for some assistance. They've got a little trouble at one of their forts and they want us to come in and give them a hand. Considering how cooperative they've always been with the Federal Marshal Service, I don't see how we can refuse."

Longarm lounged in a chair across the desk from his boss. He had it tilted back against the wall and was idly smoking a cheroot and dropping the ashes on the floor. He said, "Well, Billy, that sounds like a pretty fair proposition to me. God knows that I've used enough of their horses and enough of their supplies. Is it something here locally?"

They were in Billy Vail's office in Denver, which was the headquarters for the district.

"No," Vail said, "it's not that local, Longarm. I think you'll be taking a little trip."

Longarm brought his chair to the floor with a thump. "How long of a trip? I just got back from one. I'm due a little relaxing and laying around time. I don't mind law work, but does it always have to be at such long range?"

Vail laughed. "Don't you want to live up to your nickname of Longarm? The long arm of the law? Why, Custis, you're the most famous deputy marshal in the country."

Longarm said, "Billy, turn me over. You've buttered me well enough on this side."

Billy Vail chuckled. He was a man with thinning gray hair. He and Longarm had a running battle about each other's ages. Vail would never admit to more than forty-five, even though Longarm had accused him of being well past retirement age. "I'm sorry you said that, Custis. It was absolutely unnecessary considering the favor I'm going to do you, knowing how you like to travel in this particular area."

Longarm looked wary. "Just tell me gently."

Billy turned in his swivel chair and put both of his arms on his desk, locking his hands together. "Our friends at Fort Concho are having a little trouble. They need a first-class lawman to come down there and straighten things out."

At the mention of Fort Concho, Longarm's face fell. "Oh, my God, Billy. No . . . don't tell me that. First of all, I don't ever want to go back to Texas. Secondly, Fort Concho is in San Angelo, and that is the worst place in the world. My God, I could live the rest of my life and never go near San Angelo. That place is as dry as a whore's kiss and about as sincere. Those people that live there have been trying to scratch a living out of that hardscrabble ground so long, they have all turned as

2

tight and as mean as a wildcat eating green persimmons. Don't say Fort Concho to me and damn sure don't say San Angelo to me. Hell, Billy. No!"

Billy put up a placating hand and said, "Just hold on, just hold on. This one is important. You are the perfect man for it."

"I cannot think of anything happening in San Angelo, Texas, that would be important enough to rate even a glimmer of my attention."

Billy Vail went on earnestly. "Custis, they've got about a hundred and ten, hundred and twenty men and officers in garrison there. To refresh your memory, Fort Concho was established in 1850, back during the Indian troubles, and has been there ever since, part of a chain of forts along the southern edge of Texas and on into New Mexico and Arizona. Well, things have been pretty quiet until lately. They've had five soldiers killed there in the past two months."

Longarm said, "I don't want to appear unsympathetic, Billy, but what the hell does that have to do with me? If you're a soldier, you got a chance at getting killed, and if you're a soldier at an Indian fort, you got an even better chance."

Billy slapped the flat of his hand on the top of his desk. "Aw, hell, Custis, Don't talk nonsense. There hasn't been any Indian trouble in that country in ten years, and besides that, these soldiers were not killed in the line of duty. Custis, somebody has been murdering soldiers at that fort."

Custis got out another cheroot and lit it. It was a small, cheap cigar. It wasn't his preference. But sometimes he felt like being noble and denying himself the luxury of the long panatellas he liked.

3

"Murdering, Billy? They've been murdering soldiers? More than likely, they committed suicide just because they couldn't get out of the damn place. If anybody killed them, it was because the soldiers discovered the *one* sprig of grass growing around there, or maybe the *one* drop of water still left in the damn place, and the civilians wanted it for themselves. Why would civilians want to murder soldiers anyway?"

Billy Vail shook his head. "I don't know. That's the strangest part of it. You would think that a town like San Angelo, being no bigger than it is—what is it, around five thousand?"

Longarm nodded. "Maybe a little bigger."

"Well, you would think that a town like that would want soldiers hanging around there spending their pay, but the town has been on a tear to get that post moved. They've written congressmen, they've complained. It doesn't make a damn bit of sense, but there it is. And now, here come these murders."

"Well, why in hell didn't the army just shut down the fort and move them if the town didn't want them there. Like you said, there hasn't been any Indian trouble around that country since Lord knows when. The Comanches have been staying on the reservations and the Apaches are all in New Mexico—western New Mexico at that. Why doesn't the army just move them?"

Billy Vail said, "Where? When you've got a bunch of soldiers on the payroll, you've got to keep them somewhere. You can't keep them all in Washington, D.C. You've got a fort, you've got to put soldiers in it. Hell, Custis, don't you know anything?"

"I know that I don't want to go to San Angelo and find out who's murdering soldiers."

"Well, you're going and that's that."

Longarm got a grieved look on his face. "Why me? Tommy Wharton hasn't left Colorado in six months that I know of. He's been lapping it up in every saloon from Denver to Colorado Springs. How about Wesley Coker? Now, there's a man who oughta go to San Angelo. Hell, yes, Wesley Coker. If anybody deserves to go to San Angelo, it's Coker, and they deserve him too."

Billy Vail shook his head warily. He had expected this reaction. Truthfully, Longarm had been catching the hard assignments of late, and Vail had hoped to give the man some time off, but the request from the War Department was not to be ignored.

"Custis, I am sending you because you're the best man for the job. There is no other reason and nothing you say is going to change my mind."

Longarm looked decidedly agitated by the statement. He couldn't really tell Billy Vail why he very much did not want to go at this particular time. As far as that went, he would not have wanted to go at any time, but it was inconvenient in the here and now, and especially detrimental to a situation he had invested a good two weeks in. There was a young widow who had recently come to town. A comely young lady named Shirley Dunn whom he had been carefully cultivating since he had returned to Denver from a hard trip into the Oklahoma Territory.

This Mrs. Dunn had been coming along nicely, and he had great hopes that their friendship was about to burst into passion, but he didn't think that the iron was quite hot enough to strike yet. It wasn't anything that he was going to tell Billy Vail, however. So all he could do was carry on about the injustice of sending him out so soon on what sounded like a long and dreary and probably fruitless assignment in a part of the country that Longarm found distasteful.

He said, "Billy, you can't even get a decent drink of whiskey in west Texas. You're a drinking man. You know how that can affect a lawman's performance, his all-round general frame of mind."

Billy gave him a dry look. "Take a good supply of the Maryland whiskey that you value so much."

Longarm looked disgusted. "Why can't the army handle this for themselves? Hell, they're in the killing business. If they've lost five of them, their own soldiers, that's damn careless."

Billy Vail said, "They've asked for our help, Longarm. Now I want you to get yourself ready to go."

"Well, it just looks to me that the government ought to have some branch or body that could tend to that sort of thing."

Billy said dryly, "They do. Us. Now you can wiggle all you want to, Custis, but you're not going to get loose from this job. I'll give you a few days to get ready, but I want you gone before the end of the week. I want you in San Angelo next Monday."

Longarm sighed, his mind on the Widow Dunn, wondering if the affair could be pushed into a gallop from a sedate trot. He said, "Well, how have these so-called murders been occurring? Have we got any details?"

Billy Vail pushed a piece of paper across the desk at him. "Read that. It's the official report requesting our assistance."

Longarm took the paper, headed by the insignia of the War Department, Department of the Army, and when he was through he said, "Well, it's kind of a mixed bag. Four were shot and one was knifed. All of them occurred off post, and it appears that all of them were either on their way into town for some fun and frolic or else coming back."

Billy Vail said, "The one that was knifed in the back alley behind the whorehouse might not be connected to the others. There's no way to tell. But as to the four men that were shot, each one of them was alone, each one of them was between the fort and the town, and each one of them was killed at night. There's no doubt that they were bushwhacked."

Longarm said, "I can see that. Billy, this doesn't make a damn bit of sense. I mean, what are all these soldiers doing that the town folks would be so interested in them getting on out of there? Are they a rowdy bunch? Are they going around raping the pastor's daughter? Are they singing too loud in church?"

Vail said, "That's the puzzle. That's why I want you to go down there. I don't know any more than what's in that report. I cannot imagine the soldiers being a nuisance or a threat to the town, since that's never been a part of the town's complaint. The only complaint that has been made officially from the town's officials, and that's the mayor and the city council, is that the soldiers are no longer necessary and are taking up space that could be used for grazing and ranching. Of course, that doesn't make a hell of a lot of sense either because the army reservation is not that big."

Longarm sighed. It was a bitter pill to see the long rest that he had anticipated in the company of the lovely Shirley Dunn coming to such an abrupt and unwelcome end.

He asked, "Well, just what am I supposed to do? Go in there as a deputy U.S. marshal and start nosing around?"

Billy Vail gave him a disgusted look and said, "Yes, why don't you do that, Custis. And while you are at it, why don't you run a notice in the newspaper asking the party or parties who are murdering those soldiers to please turn themselves in to you."

Longarm said mildly, "Billy, you ought not to upset yourself like that. A man of your age . . ."

"You never mind my age. I halfway thought of maybe sending you in there as a soldier."

"As a soldier? Billy, I forgot all I knew about being a soldier."

Billy said, "I was thinking about sending you in as a buck recruit, brand-new to the army."

Longarm gave him a look. "That would probably make me the oldest recruit in the history of the cavalry."

Vail said, "One of these days we are going to track down your real age. I've looked through your records and you may not be old enough for this job, some of the things that you put down. No . . . I want you to go in there without your badge."

"Just go in as a private citizen? What's my story?"

"I don't care." Vail shrugged. "Go in as a horse trader, go in as a gambler, go in as somebody just passing through. Go in as somebody prospecting for gold. Hell, think of something, Longarm. Do I have to do all of your thinking for you?"

Longarm said, "One thing's for damn sure—I am taking my own horse. Maybe I'll take two horses with me. I'm sure as hell not gonna ride any of those rawboned hides that the army furnishes."

"Then you'll buy their tickets on the train. The marshal service is not paying for any more of your horse-trading deals. Every time you leave with one bunch, you come back with a larger bunch. If you don't want to use what the army will furnish you there, then you can damn well pay to transport your own animal or animals, however many you care to take."

Longarm shrugged. "That is uncommonly unfair of you, Billy. Now you are going to make me work to figure out some way to make up the difference on some other part of my expense report."

Billy Vail looked disgusted. "Get out of here, you big thief. Sometimes I don't know which side of that damn badge you are on."

Longarm said, "I knew that you were fond of me, Billy, but I didn't know just how fond."

"You can have yourself a little fling with that dressmaker, but you check in with me before you leave."

Longarm looked startled. "How do you know about Mrs. Shirley Dunn?"

Billy Vail said, "I am in the law-enforcement business, remember? I am supposed to know what is going on. You ain't the hardest lothario in the county to keep up with. I would have bet long odds that you'd be the first one in line the minute that woman stepped off the train. Now why don't you get on out of here and tend to your fun and frolicking and get it all out of your system in time to go to work."

Longarm put on his hat, a gray, wide-brimmed felt model that he had paid $24.95 for and was his pride and joy. He said, "Billy, you treat me too harshly."

Billy Vail said, his voice dead serious, "I wouldn't treat this one real lightly. Whoever is killing these soldiers is not exactly running on a straight set of tracks.

Somebody down there is either nuts or they have a real mean streak in them. I'd be as alert and as awake as you can get."

Longarm gave him a little salute and went out the door.

Chapter 2

He hadn't bothered to ask Billy Vail how long he could expect to be in San Angelo because he had known in advance what the answer would be. The answer would be for as long as it took, and that could be a day, a week, six months, or a year. The very thought depressed him so much that he went immediately to a saloon near the Federal Building and treated himself to several drinks of the fine Maryland whiskey that they stocked especially for him.

When Longarm was through with the saloon and somewhat reconciled to the situation, he walked down to the train depot to check the schedule that would get him to San Angelo. It took the ticket agent a few moments to figure out his route, but when he was through, it appeared that Longarm had no choice. If he were to be in San Angelo by Monday morning he had to leave Saturday. He swore softly under his breath.

The ticket agent looked up at him. "Is something wrong, Deputy Long?"

Longarm sighed. "No, Frank. Everything is just fine. A man in the law business ain't supposed to get nothing, have nothing, or want nothing. Dammit."

The ticket agent said, "You got troubles?"

Longarm turned away from the counter. "No, I don't have any troubles. I don't have anything. Listen, I'm going to need a half stock car to haul two horses."

"Is that gonna be on the government voucher?"

Longarm said, a trace of bitterness in his voice, "No, I'll be paying for that, but the government will pay for my ticket."

"Yes, sir."

Longarm left the depot and walked back toward the center of town. Off on a side street was the small dressmaking establishment of Mrs. Shirley Dunn. They had an engagement planned for Saturday night that he was now going to have to break. There was to be an evening of entertainment at the opera house and he had invited Mrs. Dunn to go. She had graciously accepted. He had anticipated that an evening of fun, aided perhaps by a champagne supper at the Brown Hotel, might lead to far more pleasant recreation. Now he stood in front of her little shop feeling miserable. It would have been their fourth formal outing. Twice they had gone dancing and twice they had had dinner at the elite Brown Hotel, Denver's finest. On two other occasions, they had met on her front porch on a Sunday afternoon, drinking lemonade and making light talk. His progress had been slow and carefully planned because Mrs. Dunn was a demure lady of breeding and delicate sensibilities. He had progressed no farther than putting his arm around her waist on a few occasions and one light good-night kiss.

Longarm was an old experienced hand at tracking the feminine species. He knew the kind that could be hurried and he knew the kind that required proper courtship. Mrs. Dunn, he was absolutely certain, was of the latter. To attempt to rush her would be to throw the game away. He suspected she could be as flighty as any deer he had stalked. And now this very unwelcome interruption had come into his social life. All he could do was go into her shop and break the news, and hope that some other buck hadn't invaded his territory by the time he got back. It was a sad errand, and he silently cursed Billy Vail as he turned the door handle and entered the little shop.

Shirley Dunn was behind the little glass counter where she sold ready-made items. The main work of her business, that of custom dressmaking, was done in the back room where she employed three seamstresses.

As he entered the store, she had her back to the door putting some boxes of lace handkerchiefs in place. She turned as he came in and said, "Oh!" putting her hand to her throat in a dainty little gesture.

She was so petite, so delicate, so proper that she always made him feel like a big shambling idiot. He took off his hat as he walked toward her, uncomfortably aware of how loud his boots and spurs sounded on the floor of the shop.

He said, "Mrs. Dunn, my, you are as pretty as a ceramic pussy cat . . . no, make that a crystal cat."

She colored prettily. "That may be the most unusual compliment that I have ever heard. At least I will take it as a compliment."

He said, "Believe me, ma'am, there is nothing else that I could pay you except a compliment. If I had it, I would pay you a million dollars just to stand here and

13

look at you, but I reckon that you will have to wait for your money."

She laughed. "Oh, Custis, how you do go on. I am surprised to see you in a ladies' shop in the middle of the afternoon. Have you come to see me or are you shopping?"

His face fell. He worked his hat in his hands in agitation. "The sad truth of it, ma'am, is that I will not be able to escort you to the entertainment Saturday night. My work calls me away."

"Oh," she said. She put her hand to her throat again. She was wearing a light gray tailored suit with a ruffled blouse that was open at the throat.

He could see the disappointment in her face, but it quickly cleared.

She said, "I am so sorry to hear that, but I can understand that someone in your line of endeavor has little control over these things."

He said, "You may rest assured of that. I am badly disappointed, ma'am. I was so much looking forward to Saturday night, but I have to be on a train Saturday morning, and by Saturday night I will be somewhere on my way to Texas."

"Texas! Oh, that is a long way."

He made a face. "Too long for me. Any place in Texas is too long for me."

"You don't care for the state?"

He said, "Ma'am, you generally don't care for places where you get shot at and knifed at and made to feel extremely unwelcome, but that is part of my business and I don't want to burden you with it. I just stopped by to tell you what I had to say." He took a step closer to the counter. "You can't believe how disappointed I am."

She put her hand out toward his. He reached to take it. She said, "So am I, Custis. Very much so. I'll miss your company, not just the entertainment."

He nodded. "I don't know how long I will be gone."

She said, "We can do it when you get back."

He tried for a smile. "I don't want any of these other fellows around here beating my time."

She smiled. "Why, whatever do you mean, Marshal?"

"You know good and well what I mean, Mrs. Dunn. A lady of your style and beauty will not lack for suitors. I fear to leave my range unattended—I fear cattle thieves, I fear rustlers."

She blushed. "My, my. What a comparison, Marshal Long."

He took her hand a little tighter and held it for a moment. Then he released it and put his hat on. "Well, I reckon I better be on about my business. You have a shop to run."

He took a step backwards, and was about to turn for the door when she said, "Custis, why not Friday night? Do you have plans Friday night?"

He turned back quickly toward her. "No, nothing that is important."

She said, "Then, perhaps you would allow me to cook you supper at my house Friday night. I'd hate to think of you going off to some dreadful place that you don't want to go to without an enjoyable evening the night before."

His heart leapt. As he looked at the swell of her breasts and the flare of her hips, thinking in his mind's eye how delicious they would look free of the constricting material of her clothes, he said, "Mrs. Dunn, that is a fine idea. I cannot think of anything that I could possibly enjoy more."

15

"Then it is settled. You will come to my house and we shall eat supper. I am a good cook, you will be surprised to know."

He shook his head. "No, ma'am, there is nothing about you that would surprise me. What time shall I arrive?"

She said hesitantly, "Would seven o'clock be too late? The shop here . . ."

"No, no, no. Seven would be fine. And please, don't go to any trouble."

"It won't be any trouble."

He told her good-bye, and turned and went out the door. His spirits were lifted high despite the dismal trip to Texas before him.

He lived in a set of rooms not far from her shop and he walked there with a happy heart. He even felt so exuberant as to run up the stairs to his second-floor quarters. It was the fourth or fifth set of rooms that he had lived in in Denver since he had been assigned there years previously. It wasn't important to Longarm where he lived since he was gone so much. He could have gotten by with just one room with a bed and a place to keep what few clothes he owned. But since on occasion he did entertain visitors, mostly ladies, he had a parlor and a bedroom and a bathroom that did well enough for his needs. He suspected that sometimes his landlady, when she knew that he could be off for considerable lengths of time, would let his rooms out on a short-term basis to visiting drummers and such itinerant peddlers as came through town looking for cheap accommodations. More than once, he had found evidence of someone else's occupancy of his quarters, but he didn't really care.

By the time he got to his rooms, he was cursing himself for having called Shirley Dunn a pussy cat. He said to himself half aloud, "That was really dumb, Long, really dumb. You could have likened her to a crystal figurine or something. Why a pussy cat?"

He poured himself a drink of whiskey, sat down in a chair by the window where he could see the street below, and lit a cheroot. For a moment, he let his mind roll over the delectable Mrs. Dunn. She had light brownish hair which she wore swept up, making him hunger to see it down and displayed in all of its glory. She had smooth, regular features except for her eyes, which were large and brown. She had a cupid's bow of a mouth, which she rouged, that he was dying to give a good kissing to.

But more than the look on her face, he ached to see what was beneath the severely cut suits and frilly blouses and no-nonsense dresses that she wore. From the look of her, he knew that it would be something to see.

Longarm was very much an appreciator of women. Except for the widow of a long-dead comrade, he had never, however, kept a permanent relationship with any. It was clear to him that he would be a poor husband, not only because of his dangerous job, but also because of the extended absences and the far-flung missions that were part of his job. From marriage, it would be a simple step to children, and he didn't think that children should grow up without some benefit from their father. Billy had once joked about some imagined wife of Longarm's trying to describe her husband to the children. Billy had said he figured that the poor woman would make a botch of the job, on account of it being so long since she had *seen* Longarm that her memory had grown dim. Billy had said, "What you'll have to do, Custis, is get a whole bunch of tintypes taken of yourself regularly and have them posted around the house so that your family can remember you."

17

But in his own mind, he knew that it was more than that. There were, he reckoned, some men who just weren't cut out for marriage and he speculated that he was one. He was a man who liked to be true to whatever he promised, and if he set out to be married to one woman, then he would expect himself to be faithful, and he wasn't sure that he could put such a hardship on himself. Many a time he had been taken with this woman or that one, to the point that he'd had a quiet talk with himself about marriage. In the end, he had seen more minuses than pluses. He might intend to be faithful, but during an extended trip away from home, a trim pair of ankles or a rounded bosom might undermine all of his good intentions in the flash of a second. He knew that he was a man easily tempted by women, and he didn't see any point in putting himself to any test.

But most of all, it was his considered opinion that a man in his line of work shouldn't be married. Of the five or six friends that he had had in the law business who had been married, all had been killed. He calculated that being a man with a wife and family gave you something to think about at a time that you shouldn't be thinking about anything else—just reacting.

He figured that a man with a family was carrying extra weight that might slow him down at just the instant that he needed to be at his very fastest.

He guessed that as long as he was married to the marshal service, he would just have to be content with whatever women came his way.

Even in that, he lived by a strict code. If a woman was too naive or too inexperienced, he would not touch her. To the best of his knowledge, he had never taken a virgin in his life. The same applied to married women—

he would not invade another man's home any more than he would steal another man's horse. A woman had to be available, experienced, and interested. He also drew the line at prostitutes. He had never laid out a dime to sleep with one and had no intention of ever doing so. His view was that what he had was just as good as what a woman was carrying between her legs and that one wasn't any good without the other. He had once told a woman who had turned out toward the end of the evening to be a prostitute that he could make her a deal—he wouldn't charge her if she wouldn't charge him.

He finally concluded that sitting there thinking about women was not the best procedure for his peace of mind. In a little over forty-eight hours, he would be having supper with the luscious Mrs. Shirley Dunn. He had no idea what the evening might bring. In fact, he didn't even want to speculate on it, so with a discipline rare for him on that particular subject, he closed his mind of the fairer sex and settled down to the business of wondering why the citizens of San Angelo didn't want money-spending soldiers near their town, and especially why they didn't want them enough to set into killing them. It was the damnedest proposition that he had ever heard of and he was becoming, in spite of himself, more interested the more he thought about it.

He had no idea how he would go about his investigation. He reckoned that he would show up and have a conference with the fort commander, making him aware of his presence, and then just hang around and listen as best as he could. As far as his cover story was concerned, that offered no trouble. He could always pretend to be a horse buyer; in fact, he very often bought horses on some of his trips. That had been a bone of contention between Billy

Vail and himself for many years—the fact that Longarm would leave with one or two horses shipped at government expense and come back with four, all shipped at government expense as well. He sometimes thought that Billy Vail just didn't see the overall picture.

He didn't expect that Shirley Dunn would be a drinking lady, so he treated himself to some whiskey before he headed out for her house. He was shaved and bathed and had on his best clothes, such as they were. He had even had his boots shined by the boy down at the barbershop, and his hat had been brushed. It was July, so it was still fair light by the time he swung open the gate to her picket fence and walked up the path to her porch and knocked on the door.

She opened it and for a second, Longarm didn't recognize her. She was the same size and the face looked the same, but she was altogether a different woman. Her hair was down in long silken waves and she was wearing some sort of a green silk outfit that you might have taken for a robe except that it fit so much closer. He didn't really get much of a chance to examine her because she held the door open wide, beckoning him to come on in. He stepped across the threshold, his hat in his hand, still amazed at the transformation in this delicate woman. She led him into the parlor. As she walked, he could see that the robe-like dress was slit up one side. It came almost to her ankles but not quite, and beneath the hem of the garment, he could see that she was wearing dainty, jeweled slippers.

He said, "Well, Mrs. Dunn, this is certainly mighty obliging of you, having me over for supper." He could feel himself stammering and searching for something to say that didn't make him sound like he was a complete idiot, but he was having difficulty because he couldn't take his eyes off her and the way that the dress clung. Never before had he seen her dressed that way.

She sensed him staring at her and she smiled. "It's Chinese," she said, "I bought it a few years back in San Francisco when I lived there with my husband. I haven't had a chance to wear it since then, so I thought it would be nice to wear it now. It has a name, but I'm not sure what you would call it—I knew at one time but I've forgotten."

He said, "Well, it's mighty fetching, ma'am."

She said, "Custis, you look all confused. Sit down and let me get you something to drink."

She disappeared. He was expecting her to reappear with a pitcher of lemonade. Instead, he was shocked to see her coming back with a tray on which rested a little pitcher of water, two glasses, and a bottle of very respectable bourbon whiskey. He would have bet that not only had whiskey never passed her lips, but it had never passed her threshold either.

She set the tray down on a little table in front of the divan he was sitting on. Then she came around the table and sat next to him.

"Shall I pour for you, Custis?"

"Well, yes, ma'am. I would be much obliged if you would." He was still trying desperately to recover from the shock that she had given him, first by the way she had fixed her hair, then by the dress she wore, and now by the way she fixed his whiskey.

She poured him a good solid tumbler. She said, "I've got a feeling that you are the kind of man who takes his drink neat."

"Well, you'd be right about that, Mrs. Dunn."

She said, "Do you really feel obliged to call me Mrs. Dunn? Can't you just call me Shirley?"

He stammered a little bit and said, "Of course, Shirley. There, that came out all right, didn't it?"

She laughed. When she did, she looked much younger than the mid-thirties he had originally figured her for. She said, "I have to take a little bit of water in mine. Too much spirits make me ardent, or is that why they call them ardent spirits?"

He almost blushed. "Well, I . . . I reckon that I never put the two of them together. Ardent spirits? That's a pretty good joke, Mrs. . . . I mean, Shirley."

She mixed her drink half and half, pouring water out of the pitcher, and then held her glass up for a toast. He raised his and they clinked.

He said, "To luck."

She said, "To love."

It was one more shock in the continuing series of surprises she was throwing at him. He downed his drink in one quick swallow, shuddering a little at the hard bite of the bourbon. As soon as he set it back down on the tray, she quickly poured it full for him again.

She said, arching a brow at him, "Are you always so quick, Custis?"

He took up his glass and drank half of it. He said, "Shirley, have you got a twin sister?"

She laughed. "No, not that I know of. Why do you ask?"

He looked around. "It's just that I have the feeling that either I am in the wrong house or that you are."

She laughed again. "You think that I have to be the same person all the time? Can't a girl have a little fun once in a while?"

He took a quick gulp from his glass. He said, his throat getting thick, "Oh, I am all for that, Shirley. I am really all for that. Yes, ma'am, indeed I am."

She was sitting very close to him and he was very aware of her body. He could smell the scent of her perfume, the power of the musk—a feminine musk that emanated from her. He let his right arm, which had been along the back of the divan, casually fall around her shoulders. Effortlessly, she came to him, her breasts pressing against his chest, her face uptilted. He set his glass down with his left hand while he looked into her eyes. Then he bent his head and kissed her, gently at first, and then with growing passion. He felt her hand slide around to the back of his neck. She was twisting herself so that the whole front of her body was up against him. For a second, he pulled back. His breathing was coming hard and labored. He looked down at her face—her eyes were closed, her lips slightly parted. He began to kiss her again. As he did, he let his left hand go to her back and then come around the silken cloth until he touched the side of her breasts. He could tell that she was wearing nothing underneath the Chinese dress. He could feel her breasts growing and swelling under his hand. He could feel the nipples hardening.

She was probing his mouth, and his heart was pounding, his jeans getting very tight. He was searching for a way to get his hand inside her dress, but there didn't seem to be any opening. He dropped his hand down along her thigh, trying to find the hem. The dress had ridden up on her until it was just below her knees. He put his hand inside, touching her cool, smooth flesh. At the very instant that he started to move his hand up the inside of her thigh, she broke the kiss off and moved backward immediately.

She said, "Why, Marshal Long. Whatever do you think you are doing?"

He said, stammering a little, "I thought you knew what we were doing. Wasn't just me, Shirley."

She said, "Custis, I think that you are being a little presumptive. You told me that you were leaving on a long trip."

He said, "Well, I don't know how long it's gonna be . . . it could be a week, could be two weeks, maybe a little longer."

"But you are going on law work, aren't you?"

He said, "Well, uh . . . yes. Yes."

"That's dangerous." She said it matter-of-factly, as if it were a statement that needed to be out in the open.

He was so taken aback that he was still fumbling for words. He said, "I suppose that one could consider it that, yes, I suppose so. Shirley, what is going on here?"

Very primly she sat on the couch and inched away from him, smoothing down the skirt of her silken dress. "Well, Marshal. A girl has got to look after herself. No one else is going to protect the future of a widowed young woman. Here you would come around and take advantage of me, and you going off on some sort of dangerous job. My husband was a man in a dangerous career—he was a gambler at cards, at horse racing, and now I end up a dressmaker. No, thank you."

He sat there stunned. He didn't know what to say. Finally, a few words tumbled out. "Shirley, you can't just lead a man on like this. I mean . . . it's not healthy. Good heavens, you've got me all worked up here. I'm as lathered up as a horse . . . a horse that has been run three miles."

She said primly, "Well, that's not my doing, is it?"

He looked around. "Well, I'll be damned if I see any other woman in the room."

"And I suppose you didn't have something in mind yourself? I suppose I planted the idea in your mind?"

He said, motioning, "Well, the way you've got yourself up and the way you received me, if I hadn't had something on my mind before, I damn sure would have five minutes after I got here."

She said, "Why don't you have another drink while I go and see to supper? It's chicken. I hope you like chicken."

He watched her get up and cross the room, his mouth hanging open. He said, "Well, yes. Of course, I like chicken. Of course, there's something I like much better."

She turned at the kitchen door and smiled at him. "But you're not going to have that."

"Would you just as soon I left?"

"Oh, no. No, you can't leave. Not after I've gone to all this trouble."

"But, what is going to happen? We're going to eat supper, but then what?"

She gave him a very impish smile with her full-lipped mouth. "I'm going to show you what will be waiting for you when you come back safely from your dangerous mission. Perhaps then you will view me in a different light and think of me more seriously." With those words she pushed open the swinging kitchen door and disappeared.

He sat there very thoughtfully. He poured himself out another drink of the bourbon and sipped at it. He knew where the misunderstanding was between himself and Shirley Dunn. She wanted him to understand that she was the marrying kind and not just some toy to be played with at his leisure. He couldn't blame her for that, not in the slightest. And he couldn't blame her for not wanting to become involved with a man who was indeed in a dangerous profession. If one husband had died violently, she wouldn't want to be involved with another who ran the same risk. He had no answer to those questions. One thing he could have told her, but hadn't, was that he was not interested in getting married. It didn't make him feel guilty given the circumstances, but he decided it was going to be very definitely an unusual night.

Just how unusual he didn't realize until she called from the kitchen, "Go and wash your hands. I'll be putting supper on the table in just a very few moments. There is a little washroom just on the back porch straight down the hall in front of you."

He did as she directed, pumping water into a basin, washing his face and hands with soap, and drying them on a big fluffy towel. After that, he walked back into the dining room area and looked at the table. It was set for two. He noticed she had particularly fine china and crystal. Her husband must have been a pretty good gambler, he thought to himself.

He was just about to take a seat, when the kitchen door came open and she backed through carrying a small tray in each hand. As she turned around and came around the door, his mouth fell open. She was wearing nothing but a small half apron, a chintzy little affair that was rounded and only went halfway down her thighs and was tied just below her navel. His first amazement was at the size of her breasts. She was one of those little women who have much bigger breasts than you expect. They were easily the size of half cantaloupes. They looked firm and uplifted. The nipples were big and the rosettes were pink and round as silver dollars. He stood there staring. She smiled at him as

26

she set the platters on the table. She said, "Why Marshal, haven't you ever seen fried chicken before?"

He swallowed, the words that had been about to come out sticking in his throat. "Yes, ma'am. I've seen fried chicken before. I just never seen it dressed quite so nicely."

She smiled again. "Well, let me get one more thing and then we'll be ready to eat. You go ahead and sit down."

But he didn't. He just stared as she turned. From the back she was completely naked. And he stood there enjoying the sight until she had disappeared through the swinging door of the kitchen. Then he finally did sit down. To the best of his knowledge he had never had supper, or any other meal for that matter, with a naked or nearly naked woman. Maybe he'd sat in bed with one and gnawed on a steak bone or had a piece of cake on a saucer, but he'd never sat down at the table with a lady dressed, or undressed, as she was. He was not at all certain he would be able to eat.

And then she came back through the kitchen door carrying a pitcher of iced tea. She sat down and gave him a bright smile while he stared at her. She said, "Now Marshal, don't be bashful. Just help yourself."

In a husky voice he said, "Ma'am, I sure wish you meant that the way I want it to be meant."

She smiled and started piling his plate with fried chicken. "Well, you just come back from your mission knowing what you have waiting for you, and then we'll have a talk and maybe you can have anything you want for supper."

He said, his voice still hoarse, "Shirley, you got any idea what you're doing to me?"

She was putting coleslaw on his plate. She said, "Of course I have an idea of what I am doing to you. I was a married woman, remember?"

"Then more the shame for you," he said.

"Bah . . . I know what your plans are, mister. They just didn't work out the way you wanted them to. I have my own plans. You're a very appealing man, Marshal Long. You have a good future. You have a good job. You're just the kind of man that I could set my cap for if there wasn't so much danger in your job. But I think that you've got enough time in the marshal service that you could have some of that danger taken out of your life."

He didn't like that. "Shirley, I don't come with conditions. There ain't no lead ropes on me. You don't see any halter around my head."

She leaned over until her breasts were almost touching her own empty plate. She said, "I'm open to compromise. Like I say, when you come back we'll talk about it. Now eat your supper."

It was undoubtedly the strangest meal that Longarm had ever tried to eat. The food was wonderful but he couldn't taste it. It seemed that all of his senses were concentrated in his eyes, which were glued to Shirley Dunn's beautiful breasts. He ate mechanically, never taking his eyes off her. He never knew if he had a mouthful of coleslaw, or mashed potatoes, or fried chicken. She served peach cobbler for dessert and asked him if he wanted cream on top. He didn't know his answer, and he didn't know if he had cream on top or not. When the meal was mercifully over they sat back down on the couch, which was even worse. For now he had a full view of her slender shapely legs. And every now and then a brief glimpse of the silken patch that was hidden by the crinkly apron. She had kept on her green slippers, and they even added to the seductiveness of the figure she cast. He had two more drinks, barely conscious of what he was doing. They talked. She asked him questions about the marshal service and his job. He answered. Sometimes he knew what he was saying, but most times he didn't. When the clock struck ten he got up and put on his hat. She walked him only partway to the door, then put her mouth up to be kissed. He kissed her long and lingeringly, but he kept his hands strictly on the smooth creamy skin of her back.

As he started to the door she said, "Just remember, I'll be waiting when you get back."

He said, "I'm gonna be remembering that you said that I could have anything for supper I wanted."

She smiled sweetly. "Under certain conditions."

He nodded. He had an idea what those conditions were and already his mind was scheming, thinking of a way around them, around whatever barriers she might put up, that would allow him to get to that luscious body.

He went out the door backwards, making sure that he had a good full vision of her to carry him all the way to San Angelo, Texas, and back.

Once out into the night air, he shook his head and said to himself, "I feel like I've been whipped with a wagon tongue and then dragged about ten miles." In truth, part of his body was convinced that another part had ceased functioning. He walked straight to his nearest favorite saloon and contented himself with a game of poker and more whiskey. But try as he would he couldn't keep his mind on the game, and ended up losing forty dollars— an almost unheard-of occurrence for him in such a low-stakes game.

But walking back to his boardinghouse that night, he got to thinking his situation over, and after a time he began to laugh. The woman had neatly turned the tables on him. He had gone there with one thing and one thing only on his mind. She had known it and what she had done was call his hand and raise the ante, letting him have just enough of a peek at his hole card to make him want to continue the game even more.

Thinking on the whole evening, he decided that it was about as clever a performance he had ever run up against. The woman wasn't just as pretty as a speckled pup, she was pretty damned smart on top of that. He reckoned when he got back, they might have some pretty good times sparring around. He had no more intention of getting married or getting serious than he'd ever had. He knew that was her intention and that she had no plans to end up his plaything. It would be curious to see if they could find some middle ground where they could meet. He got to his boardinghouse and went upstairs with a smile on his face. He was even more anxious than ever to get to San Angelo, get his business done, and get back here to the Widow Dunn.

Chapter 3

After a long, hot, tiring journey, the train finally pulled into San Angelo, Texas. For the last eight hours, since six that morning, he had had a good view of the baking plains of west Texas. He got off the train wondering just how many people in the place had actually ever seen a tree, or a stream of clear running water. But that was none of his affair. They wanted to live in such a place—he was glad that *someone* was willing. For his part, he'd have rented the whole shooting match out to Mexico for a price of one dollar a year, and if they drove a hard bargain, he'd come down from that.

He walked back along the platform toward the freight part of the train. He'd brought two horses—a gentle mare that he figured to use around town and a big rawboned chestnut that could go all day just in case he had to do some hard riding over the rough countryside. He had his saddlebags over his shoulders. They were mainly loaded with his extra .44-caliber Colt revolver, several boxes of ammunition, and five bottles of Maryland whiskey that he had brought with him from Denver, knowing full well that he'd find nothing but rotgut in San Angelo. He carried in his hand a small valise with a few changes of clothes and some fresh socks. Longarm didn't see the point of underwear in the summer. It was his opinion that, under the right circumstances, it would just slow a man down.

He arrived at the cattle car just as they were unloading the bay and chestnut. He had left the saddle on the gentle bay filly. Now he took the bridle where it was flung over the saddle, fitted it into her mouth, and cinched up the saddle. He put his saddlebags on the back, tied his valise to the saddlehorn, and climbed aboard. He had the chestnut on lead, and he started in to San Angelo. They had one decent hotel, the Cutler House. He had stayed there before and though it wasn't much, it was better than any of the boardinghouses or staying out at Fort Concho. He figured to get a suite of rooms and spread himself as much as he could. He had drawn two hundred dollars worth of expense money over Billy Vail's strong objection, and had brought along another two or three hundred dollars for gambling or horse-trading money. As far as that went, either horse he had was for sale or trade when he no longer had use for them.

San Angelo was a town that, if you took in the shacks that stretched out from the center a couple of miles, had somewhere around seventy-five hundred people in it. Why, he could never figure. There was one long, dusty, main street where most of the commerce was, and then some branching streets that had a few stores and a few shops and places where you could get this or that fixed. On beyond that were more residences and livery stables, and then you got into the shacks, and then you got into the prairie. Why anyone in the world would want to protect the place, especially the United States government, was beyond his knowledge, but then he was just a deputy U.S. marshal and he didn't have to know the why of things in order to do his job.

San Angelo was famous for one thing—it had one of the biggest whorehouses in west Texas. It was first class in operation and was run by a lady named Mabelle Russell. He'd met her on a couple of occasions, though he doubted that she would remember him. She was a handsome, elegant woman who just happened to be in the whore business. He didn't know, but he didn't think that she had come up through the ranks. He figured she was a non-participating owner, and the curious thing about it was that her whorehouse occupied the top floor of the three-story Cutler House. She took up every room on the third floor. Of course, that was with the help and the blessing of the local law, as it was considered illegal in most Texas communities for open prostitution to go on within the city limits. But like most frontier towns, the rules there were whatever the local people cared to make them.

As he went jogging down the main street leading the chestnut, he noticed that the men hadn't gotten any friendlier-looking and the women hadn't gotten any prettier. That drew his mind back to the luscious Shirley Dunn—a vision that he was doing his best to keep out of his mind until it was time to go home.

His badge was in his pocket, and it would stay there until such time as he had to take it out. He wasn't, though it normally was his habit, even going to advise the local sheriff of his presence. As far as anybody knew, or would know, he was just an itinerant gambler who would trade a horse with you or run a horse race with you or take a drink with you. A man of the world and a man on the move—no ties and no intention of being tied. He pulled his horses up in front of the Cutler House, stepped down, dropped the reins of the little bay mare, and went into the hotel.

At the desk, a young man with more mustache than his face would support said, "Yes, sir, can I help you?"

Longarm asked for a suite of rooms, preferably on the first floor. He did not know why, but on this particular occasion, he had the feeling that the time might come when he would want to make an impression. It was a hunch, and he very often followed his hunches without questioning them.

The clerk allowed as to how he did have such a suite. In fact, it was right at the end of the hall, right next to the main bathroom on the floor. He also added that it would be four dollars a day.

For answer, Longarm took out a roll of bills, peeled off a twenty, and flipped it on the desk. "There. That's for five days," he said. "Now, I have two horses out in the front. Have somebody take care of them." He put down another five. "That ought to take care of you and whoever is taking care of the horses. Now, give me my key and point me in the right direction."

The desk clerk came alive. "Yes, sir," he said with alacrity. "Yes, sir." He turned his head and yelled, "Todd! Todd, get out here and take of this gentleman's horses! Hurry up!" Then he turned to the cubbyholes behind him and took out the key that said 106 and handed it over to Longarm. Then he said, "I want you to enjoy your stay with us, sir. Breakfast is served at six in the morning, dinner at noon, and supper they commence serving at five."

"Thank you," Longarm said dryly. "I can't wait for some of that good dining-room food here at the Cutler House." He started to turn away and then looked back. "Mabelle Russell still running things up on the third floor?"

The clerk's face lit up. "Oh, are you acquainted with Miss Russell?"

Longarm said, "I reckon you could say that we know each other. Thank you."

He turned and walked away, having deliberately left the clerk with the impression that he was someone to be reckoned with. He wanted that word to get around. His intentions were to cause as much stir as he could so that he could draw more people in. That was part of the reason for the flashy roll of money, the suite of rooms, and the question about the madam. To cut a swath, he'd decided, was the way to do it. Attract some attention. Get some people talking. He didn't want to appear to be a man who would be the slightest bit interested in killing soldiers, and therefore, for that reason, he would most likely hear all about it.

He let himself into his suite. The first room had a dilapidated-looking velveteen settee and a couple of ordinary armchairs around a table. It wasn't much of a room. The only good feature about it was that it had a big chandelier over the table that had several lanterns. If a man wanted to have a poker game in private, he would have plenty of light to see his cards by.

He walked on into the bedroom. It was large enough, with a bureau and a washbasin and towels on a long table. The bed was of a fair size. He went over and felt it. It was a little lumpy but it wasn't too soft, so he figured that it would do. There was a chiffonnier to hang some clothes in, and in the corner was an ample zinc bathtub. It appeared that he could shave and have a bath in his room without bothering with the communal bathroom in the hall. He put his saddlebags down on the bed and set his valise on the floor. Then he took out a bottle of whiskey from the saddlebags and took a pull straight from the bottle, even though there was a glass handy on the nightstand just at the head of the bed.

He took out a cheroot and lit it and sat there thinking. He supposed that the first order of business was to go out to the fort, see the commander, and get a line on the killings. But just as he was about to take another pull of whiskey, there was a knock at the door and he yelled, "Come in!"

The outer door opened and a boy of about sixteen came through, carrying his .44-caliber Model 73 Winchester carbine that had been in his saddle boot.

The young man said, "Didn't figure you wanted this left out in the stable, mister."

Longarm nodded. "I expected you to bring that in, sonny. I saw you outside and I figured that you were as smart as paint. I wanted to see if I could depend on you. Here's another fifty cents for your trouble. You're supposed to get a dollar from the desk clerk. Did you?"

The young man looked doubtful, as if he was unsure of what he should answer. Longarm said, "Cheated you, did he? What did he give you, a quarter?"

The young man grinned sheepishly and looked down. "Well, I don't like to say."

Longarm added another half-dollar to what he was handing the young man. He said, "I'm going to need someone I can trust around here to run errands and help me on different matters. Would you be available for that job?"

The young man's face brightened up. "Yes, sir. I'm your man. My name is Todd."

"Now, a man that works for me has got to know how to keep things under his hat. Are you good at that?"

The young man nodded his head vigorously and said, "Yes, sir. Yes, sir."

"All right, Todd. The first thing that I want you to do is to get me a line on all the sports in town. I'm a man who is willing to get into a card game if the stakes are right, might even run a horse race, might even trade a horse. Might even buy some cattle if the price is right. Do you follow me about buying those cattle, Todd?"

"Yes, sir. I figure I do."

"Fact, I might even buy a load of horses if the price is right. Do you understand me about that, Todd?"

"Well, yes, sir, but I gotta tell you, sir, that there ain't many of them kind of horses comes through here."

"What kind of horses did you think I meant, Todd?"

"Well, sir, I kind of thought that you might have meant horses that have gotten lost and cattle also."

Longarm said, "You're a smart paint, Todd. Now you run along and keep your eyes and ears open. You might put the word around to the right places that I am also a man who likes to have a good time. Do you understand me, Todd?"

"Yes, sir!" Todd said. Then he turned and was gone.

Longarm watched him close the door and then smiled to himself. He thought he could begin to enjoy this act, that is, as long as the money held out. If it didn't, he'd have to deal with the tight-fisted Billy Vail. Billy's idea of acting like a sport meant throwing around a dollar and a half. It was Longarm's considered opinion that Billy Vail ought to be the Secretary of the Treasury of the United

States of America, as tight as he was. Longarm picked up his carbine and levered it slowly to see that a shell was still in its chamber. He liked to make sure that all of his weapons were loaded, just as he liked to make sure that he never carried a dull knife.

A man had once told him early in life that it didn't cost any more to carry a sharp knife and a loaded gun. He'd added, however, that sometimes it did cost more to have a pretty woman than to have an ugly one. On that thought, Longarm had another drink and went over to look out the window at the main street of San Angelo. It didn't take him long to see that there wasn't much to see.

He moved back to the bed and unbuckled his gunbelt. He was tired from his journey and he wanted to take a rest before looking the town over. He unbuckled the big concave silver buckle of his gunbelt carefully because inside the buckle, held by a spring, was his hideout gun, a .38-caliber two-shot derringer. He didn't need it very often, but when he did, he needed it mighty bad.

He took his boots off, loosened his belt, lay down on the bed, and shut his eyes. He couldn't sleep, but he could rest for a half an hour and then go out to the fort, where he hoped to see the commander. He figured that the sooner he got to the nub of the business, the sooner he would get it over with.

The commander of the fort was a Captain John Montrose. He was a man of approximately Longarm's age, though he was tall and thin where Longarm was muscular. His face was weathered, as were his clothes. It was obvious that this wasn't his first tour of duty at a frontier fort.

Longarm managed to get into see the captain by claiming to have a bill for forage against the army that he wanted forwarded through proper channels. Once he had managed to see Captain Montrose alone, he immediately dropped the ruse, showed the captain his badge and papers, and told him the purpose of his visit.

Captain Montrose leaned back in his chair in his sparsely furnished office and said, "Well, Marshal, I have to admit that I am very glad to see you. Frankly, the entire matter is a puzzle to me. This is my fourth tour of duty at these so-called Indian forts, and nothing like this has ever happened before."

Longarm said, "Captain, I just got in town this afternoon. I've just barely had a drink and a rest. You will at least give me until supper to solve this thing, won't you?"

The captain gave him a rueful smile. "I guess when you have been living with something like this as long as we have, you are anxious for it to be over with."

"I've been told that this business started about two months ago. Is that when the first killing occurred?"

Captain Montrose nodded. "That's approximately right."

"When did the local townspeople begin to make it evident that they didn't want you around?"

The captain scratched his thinning hair. "Well, that part is a puzzle to me too. I don't really know of any concerted effort or wish to have us leave. It just seems to crop up here and there. I've been told that letters have been written to the congressman and the governor, but I've never seen any of them. I've been told that the mayor has protested our being here, but I have asked him point-blank and he says he has never made any such protest. Frankly, I am puzzled by the entire affair. I am told that the entire town wants this fort closed, and yet I can't find a single soul that will tell me that they want us gone. Asked directly, they invariably say, 'Why would we want you to leave?' And since we provide a flow of money in the form of our payroll and the amount of supplies that we buy, I couldn't imagine why the town would want us gone. I admit myself that I can't see the necessity of this fort. The only Indians that I know of around here work on cattle ranches and are very unlikely to go on a warpath anytime soon."

He smiled briefly. "We are primarily a training base. Most of my men are new recruits. We work them here and then move them on up the line to Fort Bliss in El Paso, and from there they go on into New Mexico and Arizona, where there are still some Indian fights going on. We're a threat to no one, so I am as puzzled as anyone about this."

Longarm shook his head. "Well, this gets thicker and thicker."

Captain Montrose said, "What do you propose to do?"

"There ain't a hell of a lot I can do, Captain. I'm gonna hang around and act like I am a big spender just in from the gold country. Try to stir some folks up and keep my ears open. Five soldiers killed?" Longarm shook his head. "That's a pretty strong protest. Are you sure that it wasn't personal?"

The captain shook his head. "I don't see how. The men had absolutely nothing in common other than they were all U.S. soldiers. One of them was a corporal and the other four were privates. They were from different parts of the country. Two were immigrants, as many of our men are, you know. They were young, they were middle-aged. None were vicious. No common thread that I can think of."

"What about the idea that the land that you are occupying could be used by citizens for grazing and other purposes?"

40

The captain said, "Hell, we don't take up more than two hundred acres. You can't graze much on two hundred acres around here. We do most of our training way out in the country. There's no land around here that would be considered of any value. Unless you consider that the fort, being set as close to the town as it is, is a valuable piece of property. But surely there is ample room for town expansion without leveling the fort."

Longarm got up and put his hat on. "Well, I'll get on about my business. You and I, of course, don't know each other, Captain. I will be giving you some information from time to time when I have something to report."

"You can give me no idea how long this will take?"

Longarm shook his head. "Not the slightest, Captain."

"Do you think any more of my men will be murdered?"

Longarm just gave him a look.

Captain Montrose laughed and said, "Yes, I guess that was a silly question."

Longarm rode away from the garrison back toward the town, knowing no more than when he'd ridden out. He took his horse to the hotel stable to turn him over to the stable boy. Todd was just coming out, leading a sleek-looking quarter horse.

Longarm said, "What's that you got there, Todd?"

Todd's face lit up. "Oh, this be Mr. Castle's horse, sir."

"Well, who is Mr. Castle?"

"He's a member of one of the most prominent families around here, sir. There is a bunch of them. This one here belongs to Mr. James Castle. He is an uncle of the main branch of the family."

Longarm said, "Well, just remember our deal."

He turned his horse in to the stable and then walked back toward the hotel. He went back into the hotel dining room and had supper. They gave him what they considered roast beef, which he thought was better suited to making shoes out of, along with some stuff they called gravy—he figured that you could glue the shoes together with it—along with some canned tomatoes and some mashed potatoes. He figured that he was either going to have to find a better place to eat or get some grub out of the general mercantile and start eating in his room.

That evening, he walked a few doors down from the hotel to the Elite Saloon, which was considered the biggest and the best in town. Todd had reported to him that it was at the Elite that the biggest gamblers gathered. He stood at the bar watching the play at several tables until a seat came open at a game where the stakes were high enough to interest him. There were five other players. With the exception of one man, they seemed to be ordinary-looking local cattle ranchers or townspeople in some kind of trade or another. The exception was a huge bull-necked man with a heavy thick face and small eyes that seemed to flick back and forth out of their slits.

Longarm could see the man wasn't fat, he was just big and solidly built. He judged the man to weigh pretty close to two hundred and fifty pounds. He wasn't as tall as Longarm, but he was still a stretch over six feet.

No names were given and no introductions were made. The only introduction that you needed was your fifty-cent ante and the knowledge of how to deal when it came your turn. On the first hand that he played, which was five card draw, Longarm won a thirty-five-dollar pot with three tens. On the second hand, he bought the pot with a twenty-dollar bill and a pair of jacks showing in a game of five card stud. He had made the bet on the last card up, and it had been only himself and the bull-necked man. The bull-necked man had looked at the twenty-dollar bill, and then looked at his hole card and folded. Longarm had pulled the pot in. He was playing contrary to his usual game.

He was being flamboyant, he was talking, and he was making jokes. Normally when he played, he showed no emotion and talked very little, if at all. But then, this was different. He was trying to draw attention to himself. He could see that the bull-necked man didn't like him. On the third hand, which was also five card stud, he won it straight up with a pair of kings showing, a pair of tens showing, and a ten in the hole. He had won three straight. He calculated that he was up almost a hundred dollars.

On the fourth hand, which was draw and which he was dealing, he dealt himself a pair of queens and a pair of nines. Three players stayed after the first bet, which was made by the opener to his left. Longarm drew one card, as did the bull-necked man, and immediately bet twenty dollars. He bet it casually without looking to see what he had drawn, almost as if he were taunting them. Of course, the one card draw could mean that he was drawing to fill a flush, a full house, or a straight. Or he could have been holding three of a kind with a kicker and just being cute by drawing one card. The bull-necked man kept his eyes steadily fixed on Longarm, as he had ever since the second pot. Longarm could feel an enmity radiating from him. To help it along, he directed most of his bantering remarks to the heavyset man. As he did, he noticed that the other players glanced at him uneasily as if they thought he was making a foolish play.

With a twenty-dollar bet on the table, the man who had opened hesitated and then called it. The man next to him folded, and the heavyset man took a long time debating before he finally pitched his hand in. When the cards were spread, the opener had two pairs, jacks over fours, and Longarm had made a full house—three queens over his pair of nines.

As he raked in the money, he said, "Hell, if I had known that it was this easy around here, I would have gotten here yesterday, maybe even the week before. As it is, I figure that in a year I can buy this damn town, but what in God's name I would want with it, I don't know. Unless I was a soldier and was forced to live here, I can't see no good reason for staying."

A quiet came over the table. The big man said in a rumbling voice, looking dead at Longarm, "If I were you, mister, I'd make it awhile before I win another pot. That's four pots in a row that you've won. You keep fooling around, I'm gonna mess you up good. Do you understand me? I'm gonna mess you up good. I'm gonna mess your face up."

Chapter 4

Longarm stopped stacking his chips, leaning back easily in his chair. He looked at the man. "Is that a fact? Well, how do you know that I won't appreciate it if you mess my face up? What makes you think that I like my face the way it is? It might turn out that I would be obliged to you for changing my face, 'cause a lot of folks' faces need changing. Like yours, for instance. You are nearly the ugliest thing that I ever saw. Why don't you go run into a barn door or hit yourself in the face with the flat of a shovel. That would be an improvement."

He heard a few gasps from around the table. He could hear the sound of chairs scraping back. For a second nothing happened, and then the big man slowly rose. He started to his right. The men sitting on that side of the table jumped out of their chairs and hurried back out of the way. The heavyset man didn't come with a rush. He came ponderously, heavily, with his arms out from his barrel chest. Longarm could see from the size of his arms that if the man could ever succeed in getting him in his

45

grasp, he, Longarm, would most likely be done for. He stood up slowly, giving the man time to round the table. He had a fairly good idea what the man was going to do. He stepped to his left and just hooked his chair with the toe of his boot so that he could fling it.

As the man came around the curve of the table, he suddenly started forward. In that same instant, Longarm jerked the chair into the man's path. It caused the big man to stumble. As he started to fall forward, Longarm pulled out his gun and clubbed him over the back of the head and neck. He hit him as hard as he could. The sound of the barrel striking the hard flesh made a *thunk* in the quiet of the saloon. The big man just kept falling, crushing the chair beneath him. He hit the floor on his chest and bounced and then lay still for a second.

Longarm stepped back and was about to holster his revolver, thinking it was all over. But then the big man shook his head several times and started slowly to rise.

Around him, Longarm could hear the buzz of voices. It seemed he kept hearing Billy Bob this and Big Billy that. He said to the rising man, "Stay down, mister. I am warning you . . . stay down."

The big man seemed not to have heard him. He kept shaking his head as if to clear it and slowly rose, pushing himself up with his massive arms until he was on his hands and knees. As he was about to straighten up, Longarm stepped forward and kicked him under his chin as hard as he could. The blow knocked the man over backwards. He went down and then rolled over on his right side.

Longarm stood there, watching, wondering what would come next. Once again the man lay still for a few seconds, and then once again he started to laboriously heave himself to his feet.

Longarm watched him, fascinated, as the man pushed himself up with one arm, then up on one knee, and then began to slowly straighten up. As he did, Longarm drove the heel of his right boot into the man's side. He could almost felt the crunch of a rib. The man sighed and sagged back down. Longarm booted him again. This time, the blow drove him to the floor.

The process started again, only this time, Longarm knelt beside the man and put his revolver between his eyes, cocked the hammer, and said, "Listen, you chubby little sonofabitch, stay down there on that floor or I'll put one right between your eyes. I ain't letting you squeeze the life out of me."

A voice from behind him said, "Let him alone, mister." He turned around slowly. He was looking into the twin barrels of a shotgun. Behind them was a young man who bore a resemblance to the heavyset man on the floor, only this one was taller and more normally built. But he was still heavy and he still had a bullying look about his face and little mean, cruel eyes. There was no mistaking his intent with the shotgun. Longarm looked at him. He still had the gun pointed at the man on the floor.

Longarm said, "Who might you be?"

The man said, "Never mind who I be. You let him alone."

Longarm said, "You drop that scattergun. I don't care much for having those things pointed at me."

"You take that pistol out of my brother's face."

"Your brother started this fight. Your brother don't want pistols pointed at his face? He ought to not offer

47

violence to other men. Now you put that scattergun down and I'll take this pistol out of your brother's face and I'll back out of here and we'll all just be friends for the rest of our lives. Now, what do you think of that?"

While the questions hung in the air, there was a commotion and a man came shouldering his way through. "What the hell is going on here?" he said.

Longarm was glad to see that he was wearing a badge. He hoped that it was the sheriff and not one of his deputies. He figured from the age of the man that it had to be the sheriff, and judging by his authoritative ways, he was fairly certain it was.

Someone said, "This man's been beating the hell out of Billy Bob."

Longarm looked up at the sheriff. "I wasn't beating the hell out of Billy Bob, if that's his name. I was only protecting myself. This sonofabitch that's about the size of a barn was going for me. I wasn't going to stand there and get squashed to the floor."

The sheriff looked around at the other players in the game. He singled one out and said, "What about it, Mr. Swinney?"

Mr. Swinney, who was one of the men who looked like a tradesman, sort of shrugged and said, "The new fellow won four hands in a row. Billy Bob didn't like it. He kind of mentioned to the new fellow that he didn't like it and that he was going to give him a working over."

The sheriff said, "All right, I don't give a damn about any of that. Glenn, you put that shotgun down." Then he pointed his finger at Longarm and said, "And you, mister, put that gun back in its holster, get your money off the table, and get the hell out of this saloon."

Longarm stood up slowly, uncocking his revolver before slipping it into his holster. He said, "I didn't start this fight."

The sheriff said, "I don't care who started this fight. I'm here to finish it. Now pick your money up off that poker table and get the hell out of here."

"Whether I'm ready to go or not?"

"Whether you're ready to go or not. Makes me no damn difference. I'm the sheriff here—you'll do what I tell you. Now get out of here."

At Longarm's feet, the big man groaned and moved around. Longarm glanced down. A trickle of blood was running down the thick neck from where the gun barrel had cut him at the base of his skull. Longarm looked over at the younger man who had the same features and the same blond hair—hair so blond that it was almost white. The younger man had dropped the barrel of the shotgun but his eyes were still aimed at Longarm. Longarm glanced around the room. Everyone was staring at him.

He said to the sheriff, "Just who the hell are these two gents that they would rate the law taking a position over another private citizen? I ain't done a damn thing except play a better poker game than that idiot on the floor."

The sheriff's face flushed. "Never you mind who they are or who anybody else is for that matter. Just get your damn money and get the hell out of here. My job is to keep trouble from starting and to stop it once it gets started and I don't want any more. Do I got to tell you again?"

With casual movements, Longarm stepped to the table and scooped his money up, stuffing it into his pocket. Then he glanced down at the big man named Billy Bob or Big Billy and gave him one last look. He started toward the man with the shotgun. As he shouldered his way between him and the sheriff, he said to the younger man, "Listen, sonny. I ain't real sure that you are old enough to be carting one of those things around. Ain't there some law, Sheriff, about twelve-year-old boys carrying a shotgun?"

The sheriff said, "Hold it right there, Glenn. I'll tend to this. Glenn, just put that shotgun down and step back. This man is leaving."

He took Longarm by the shoulders and gave him a nudge toward the front of the saloon. "On your way, mister."

Longarm shrugged the sheriff's hands off. He walked a few steps and then turned around and looked the room over slowly. Finally he smiled slightly, turned, and walked toward the door, making a sardonic wave over his shoulder. As he stepped through the bat-winged doors, he could hear the noise begin to pick up again in the place. Outside on the street, he laughed. It had been a good beginning. If nothing else, he told himself, he had won nearly two hundred dollars. More money to flash around and act like a sport.

He wandered the streets for a quarter of an hour, then turned a corner and went into a saloon called the Square Deal, which he thought to himself was anything but.

It was no way on a par with the Elite. It was more of a workingman's drinking place. He was about to turn around and go back out when out of the corner of his eye, at the end of the bar, he saw the blue tunics of a couple of cavalry soldiers. He walked on in. There was one poker game going and he could tell at a glance that it was small change—nothing that he wanted a part of.

He took a place at the bar and ordered a drink, making a grimace as he tasted the raw whiskey. He slammed his glass down and said to the bartender, "Hell, you slopping pigs or giving drinking men whiskey? What is this stuff? Give me something decent."

The barkeep looked startled. "Well, that's good enough for most folks around here."

Longarm slung a silver dollar on the bar and said, "Give me your best."

The bartender shrugged and found another bottle. He took a fresh glass and poured Longarm another drink. Longarm took it down in one gulp, grimacing. He said, "Hell, that ain't a hell of a lot better."

He looked down to where the two cavalry men stood. Both were slick-sleeved privates. He said, "And not only ain't the whiskey worth a damn in this joint, but you don't seem to care who you let in here. You serve soldier boys in here—Yankee soldier boys? Next you'll be letting Injuns in here to drink with the white men." He flipped another silver dollar on the bar and turned on his heels and walked out.

Out on the street, he smiled again. He was well pleased with himself. He had managed to make a stir in two places. It was growing late—a little after ten—so he walked slowly back to his hotel. As he was crossing the lobby, he saw the young man, Todd, hurrying after him. Longarm continued on down the hall. Just as he reached his room, Todd came up.

Todd said excitedly, "Mr. Long, sir. I got to tell you something."

"What is it, Todd?"

"Well, Mr. Long. I heard that you got into a . . . got into an upset with Billy Bob Castle and his brother Glenn."

"Is that their name? Castle?"

"Yes, sir. Just like the one that had the horse that you were admiring this afternoon."

"So what?"

"Well, sir. I just thought I better warn you. They ain't the best folks to be getting crosswise with around here."

Longarm put his key in the door.

The boy continued. "They're kind of pretty important around here. They're kind of the head stud horse. The whole bunch of them."

Longarm gave the young man a look. He said, "Well, Todd. You pass the word that if they will stay clear of me, I'll let them go on being stud horses around here, but they fool with me and I'll geld them right quick."

Todd stood there staring at him as Longarm went past the door, shutting it behind him. He walked through the parlor into his bedroom and sat down on his bed to have a good laugh. He uncorked a bottle of Maryland whiskey and swished it around his mouth to get rid of the taste of that last drink. He leaned back against the pillow and said, "Ahhh," before taking out a cigarillo and lighting it.

He figured that he had done a pretty good day's work in the little town in not quite half a day. He didn't know who the Castles were—Billy Bob or Glenn—but they apparently were of such a size and vigor and prestige as to have made Todd impressed with his conflict with such a robust family.

All of it had left him no closer to finding who was killing the troopers. The remark he had made in the Square Deal Saloon about the place serving soldiers was possibly the most aggressive effort he had made that day, but it would take a great deal more than that to get him viewed as an arrival who shared the town's opinion toward the garrison at the fort.

As he ate his breakfast the next morning in the hotel dining room, he reflected that if he ever meant to make his official presence known to the sheriff, the sheriff's behavior the night before had canceled out that thought. Clearly the sheriff took the side of the locals against any outsiders.

Longarm wondered if that included the soldiers at the fort. Were they outsiders since most of them were Yankees? Even worse than that, most of them were immigrants newly arrived in the country. The only work they could find was that of serving in the army, and especially in the frontier forts. Many of those forts were now being manned by Negroes who were called buffalo soldiers. As a general rule, being sent to such far-flung outposts was reserved for outcasts, the second-rate and troublemakers. Of course, that did not apply to the officers to the same extent as the enlisted men. But no matter what their social status was, they didn't deserve to be killed.

He wondered about the Castle family, and intended on making some discreet inquiries in time. He thought, however, that their paths would be crossing in the very near future. The burly man they called Big Bill or Billy Bob, or even the one they called Glenn, the one with the shotgun, didn't look like the type to take a licking and think very kindly about it. He thought for certain that they would be paying him a visit in the very near future.

But for the time being, his plan was just to hang around town and listen to what he could hear, put forth such opinions as might find favor with those who were against the soldiers being there, and let the situation take its course. He knew of no other way to proceed.

However, later that morning he received a communication from Captain Montrose. They had worked out a method of communicating by which Longarm could not be identified with the garrison. There were several civilian employees at the fort, and a blacksmith who saw to the garrison's horses was to drop off a message at his hotel. It wouldn't be a closed envelope but rather an innocent-looking piece of paper mentioning lost horses and Longarm's search for them. That would notify him that he was supposed to come to the fort as quickly as possible.

He met Captain Montrose in the horse corrals at the fort at one o'clock. The captain said that he had forgotten to mention that he was taking most of the troop on a training march the next day, and he wanted to make sure that such an action would not interfere with Longarm's investigation. Longarm told him in no uncertain terms it would very definitely interfere with his investigation.

He said, "Captain Montrose, how the hell am I supposed to find out who's shooting your soldiers if you march them out of here?"

The captain said, "But I'll be leaving a small complement of clerks and other personnel."

"Don't make no difference. You'll just slow me down during the time it takes you to carry out this exercise. How long were you planning on being gone?"

"Ten days to two weeks."

The very thought of having his mission delayed by that amount of time made Longarm cringe. In the strongest terms possible he gave it as his opinion that if the captain did such a thing, it might well cancel the progress Longarm had already made. He didn't bother to tell the captain that his progress thus far had been to get into a poker game and into trouble with the local sheriff.

Captain Montrose didn't want to comply with Longarm's wishes, but in the end he had no choice, even though he complained that it would cause his troops to lose significant training time.

Longarm said, "Better that they lose their training time than lose their lives."

With that Longarm left and headed back to town.

His first stop was the Elite Saloon. There, over several drinks at the bar, he let it be known that he was almost certain that several of his horses, horses that had been stolen, were being held out at the garrison, and that that damned Yankee captain would not release them. And he, by God, was going to have justice on the matter or there would be hell to pay. All of this he told to the bartender, who was not at all interested, but he told it to him in such a way that practically everyone in the place could hear him.

After that, Longarm ambled down the street looking for the sheriff's office. He found it right across from the Cutler House. At the same time, he discovered that the sheriff's name was T.J. Smith. His office had a plate-glass window and his name was printed across in it in large letters, showing the man was either proud of being sheriff or proud of his name, or had an overly-ambitious sign painter on his payroll.

Longarm opened the front door and stepped into the fair-sized office. The sheriff was behind the biggest of three desks. He was set up right in front of the door that obviously led back to the cells. There were two other smaller desks that were set against the wall to Longarm's left. At one of them, a young deputy was sitting with his feet up, drinking a cup of coffee. The sheriff had his hat off and was working on some papers. Longarm could see that he was going bald, and noticed the gray in the man's drooping mustache. He figured the sheriff to be pushing fifty, but he was still a solid-built man with a lined face and hard eyes. He seemed capable of enforcing his authority without too much trouble.

He looked up as Longarm walked up to his desk. For a second his eyes blinked, and then he recognized Longarm. He said, "What the hell do you want?"

Longarm glanced over at the deputy, who was watching him. He said to the sheriff, "I'd like to know where the hell you got off rousting me around last night after them two ruffians jumped on me. One was gonna squash me like a bug and the other was gonna take a shotgun to me."

The sheriff skittered his chair back away from his desk so he could look up and have a better slant at Longarm. "I don't know who the hell you are, mister, or who the hell you think you are, but those two are part of the best family in this county, so they count for a hell of a lot more than somebody that is just in here for some unknown reason. By the way, what *is* your business in my town?"

"The last time I looked, this was a free country. Unless a man done something wrong, he didn't have to explain anything to the law. But just for your information, I deal in stock and the government owes me for some horses I sold them. I have reason to believe that some of them, the ones that I didn't get paid for, are out here at this so-called fort you got. Now, you let one man cheat you and another will try it. I don't want it on my record that I let some damned quartermaster pocket my money, doctor his records, and make it look like I never sold the government some horses. I know my brands, and I'll either wind up getting my money or my horses back. That good enough for you?"

Before the sheriff could answer, the deputy dropped his boots to the floor with a thump and said, "Sheriff, don't tell me that this is that fella that took on Billy Bob last night?" He laughed and looked at Longarm. "Mister, was I you, I wouldn't be studying about no damned horses if I had Billy Bob Castle on my ass. I'd be figuring out the fastest way that I could get out of here and put the most territory I could between me and him. He'll be in town tonight and guess what? He'll be looking for you."

Longarm looked back at the sheriff and said, "Then it will be your job, Sheriff Smith, to keep him off my ass. I am a taxpaying citizen. I mind my own business."

The sheriff looked at him sardonically and said, "Well, if minding your own business includes pistol-whipping Big Billy Castle, then you'd better take up another business."

Longarm said, "Just who the hell are the Castles?"

The deputy answered first. "You ain't ever heard of the Castles? Boy, you must be from a long ways off."

Longarm's head whipped around toward him. "Son, when you get to be half my age, then you can start calling me boy, but until then, it ain't a real good idea."

The deputy laughed. "Feisty old sonofabitch, ain't ya?"

Longarm said evenly, "Feisty, yes. Sonofabitch, sometimes. Old, not yet. Watch your mouth, sonny."

The sheriff said, "You're causing nothing but commotion around here. You're not really welcome in this town."

Longarm said, "Well, welcome or not, I have business in this town and I intend on staying here until I get it tended to. Now I am a logical and a reasonable man. Do you mind telling me why I am supposed to treat these Castle folks so politely? How come they deserve the buttered side of the bread"

The deputy said, "Because they keep this area going. They have two of the biggest cattle outfits around here. They are by far the wealthiest people around. They hire more men, they spend more money. They keep this outfit going. Ya need any better answer than that? Ain't money at the bottom of most everything?"

Longarm said, "Well just who are they? Is it just one family?"

This time the sheriff answered. "The real head is old Vernon Castle. He was the first one out here. He's got three boys. You've met two of them, Billy Bob and Glenn. then there is a younger one, Virgil. He's not much into the business end of things. Then there is Vernon's younger brother, James. He's got a pretty good-size spread. He's got two young sons and two daughters. And, yes, they own just about everything that you see, including that hotel that you are staying in. So unless you want to get thrown out of there, you'd better mind your p's and q's."

"So they run the town, do they? Do they run the law also?"

The sheriff's head snapped up. "You know, I'm getting a little tired of your smart mouth, mister. How'd you like to spend a little time back there in one of those cells?"

Longarm said, "When I have done something that deserves it. You try to put me in there before that, you'll see more lawyers than you've ever seen in your life coming at you. I'm not a man without means myself. I cut a little mustard back in my own country."

"And where would that be, if it's any of my business?"

"Well, it don't happen to be any of your business, but it's Tennessee and parts of Louisiana and parts of Arkansas. Us Longs, we tend to get around. There's quite a few of us and we tend to get some people voted into office ourselves, so I understand how that works. You just make sure that the three-hundred-pound baby bull stays the hell away from me, or next time I won't use the barrel on him. I'll use it *in* him."

Before the sheriff could answer, Longarm pushed away from his desk, gave the deputy a curt nod, and walked out of the office, well pleased with himself.

Later in the afternoon, Longarm saddled up the chestnut gelding with the intention of making a reconnaissance in order to get a lay of the land. He'd gotten some rough directions from one of the stable hands as to where the two Castle ranches were located. But the country was so big that all he'd really be able to do would be to place their headquarters. They owned parcels of land in a great circle all around the town.

He also had a map that the garrison commander had drawn him showing where the five soldiers had been killed. He eliminated the one that was stabbed in the alley, considering him as not part of the pattern since the others had obviously been bushwhacked by rifle fire.

He rode out of the town toward the south, taking a road that led toward Eden, some forty miles away. He thought to name any place Eden in such country showed a remarkable sense of humor on the part of the residents. He had, of course, no intention of going some forty miles away.

His main interest was the location of Castle property in relation to where the four troopers had died.

It was a warm day and enough wind was blowing to raise the light, powdery, leachy dust that was so irritating to a man's nose. He took a big bandanna out of his saddlebags and tied it around his face like a bandit, just over the bridge of his nose. His horse wouldn't suffer because nature had put enough hair in a horse's nose so that it would filter out such trouble.

He put the chestnut into a ground-eating lope and rode in a wide eastward swath until he located the headquarters of the James Castle ranch. They appeared to be running cattle that were a mixed breed of shorthorns and whiteface Herefords with a base stock of longhorn mixed in with them. Only in the last ten years had the ranchers realized the necessity of breeding beef stock to the all-bone, longhorned cattle. The small gentle Midwestern beef stock couldn't handle the harsh Texas climates by themselves, but if they were crossed with the hardy stock of the longhorn, then you got a good bit of the longhorn's hardiness, and you put a little meat on his bones with the shorter-horned or Hereford cross.

He set his horse on the dirt road and looked out across the half mile between himself and the headquarters of the James Castle branch of the family. It was a big, two-story adobe or stucco structure with red Mexican tile on the roof. Even from that distance, he could see that it was a well-kept place, and around the barns and other outbuildings he could see men working.

He had no reason to suspect that the Castles had anything to do with the murders. It was just that they had come to his attention first, and if anyone would be interested in the welfare and management of the country around San Angelo, it would be the largest landowners, and that most definitely would be the Castle family.

He rode on, curving toward the north toward the little town of Wall, about seven miles east of San Angelo. He passed Wall and continued further north, disliking the country as much as he had from previous visits. They had done an excellent job of growing rocks, cactus, sand, mesquite trees, and a few scrub oaks, but there was damned little grass for cattle to eat and damned few cultivated crops. Here and there he saw some scraggly fields of corn, oats, and wheat, but he was damned if the country would handle more than one cow per one hundred acres. If a man was going to make a living ranching, he needed a hell of a lot of land.

The headquarters for the Vernon Castle ranch was about five miles northeast of San Angelo. The fort, he noted, lay in almost a direct line between San Angelo and the Vernon Castle ranch. It wasn't significant because as Captain Montrose had said, the government land didn't cover enough area to be worth anybody's life, much less four troopers. Still, it was interesting to note that the Castles did have parcels of land that were much closer to the fort, some that were almost bordering the government land that the fort occupied.

The Vernon Castle ranch house was very much like that of the other brother, big and white with a red-tiled roof and plenty of outbuildings and corrals and barns. It too showed the effects of money and attention.

Having seen all that he wanted to see, he turned his horse and headed back toward town. His route took him very close to Fort Concho. He thought about stopping by to see Captain Montrose, but decided that the less he was identified with the garrison, the better off it was for all concerned.

But as he rode by, the thought came to him of just how folks in the East pictured a frontier fort. Most of them thought it had a wall around it, supposedly to keep the Indians out. That wasn't the case now, nor had it ever normally been the case. First of all, there usually weren't enough building materials to build a wall around a garrison fort. Secondly, there weren't any Indians stupid enough to come and attack over a hundred soldiers on their own home grounds. The fort was a series of barracks, barns, and other buildings built around a large parade ground, or quadrangle as the army called it. He figured that the neat row of houses where the married officers lived would be a disappointment to the folks back East, who visualized the fort as being on constant alert against an Indian attack. Behind one officer's house, he could see a Mexican lady hanging clothes on a line to dry. He reckoned the woman was completely unaware that at any second some wild Indian could put an arrow through her breast. It made him laugh.

He rode on back into town over the featureless land, broken only here and there by buttes that had stood the test against nature and reared up two or three hundred feet off the flat prairie. Other than buttes and arroyos and crevices and draws that slashed the ground here and there, it was hard to tell what part of the country you were in just by looking around.

He put his horse up at the hotel stable and went back to his room. First he had a drink and then a smoke. He sat there trying to think of something smart to do, but nothing would come. What he needed was information about the people of the area, about the history of the area, and about the attitude that was prevalent toward the soldiers. There didn't seem to be any way to get that information without giving himself away as a U.S. marshal. That was the hell of it.

He couldn't use his badge for any good purpose. In this case, it was a hindrance more than a help. He didn't have the slightest idea of how he was going to go about tracking down the murderer or murderers of the soldiers. Hell, he thought, it could be anyone. Anybody could lay off the road between the fort and the town, and on moonlit nights he'd have no trouble knocking a bluecoat out of the saddle.

Of course, it was interesting, especially in view of the fact that one of the Castle ranches was to the south and another to the northeast, that while three soldiers had been killed on the road between the fort and the town, one had been shot out of the saddle south of town on the road that could be said to lead to the James Castle ranch. He didn't know if he was being influenced by the fact that he didn't like the Castle kind of people, the kind that wanted to control towns, the kind that wanted to control other people's lives. That could be entering into it, he had to admit to himself.

He decided that that night might be the time to meet with someone he figured knew everything and everybody and every detail of what was going on in town, the madam of the whorehouse up on the third floor, Mabelle Russell. The only problem with that was he could not recollect if he had ever let on to her that he was a federal officer. It had been three or four years since he had been in San Angelo and he dimly remembered being incognito back then. It hadn't been the same kind of a job, but as a general rule, unless there was a need for it, Longarm kept his badge in his pocket. He never paraded the fact that he was a marshal. If somebody was going to do something wrong, they seldom did it if they knew they were standing right next to a law officer. Besides, on a purely social basis, people tended to shy away from you when they saw that big gold and blue enameled badge. It scared them, made them think that you were the bogeyman or maybe going to put them in jail.

He decided that he would have his supper if he could find a decent place to eat, and then have a few drinks at the Elite, perhaps with the opportunity to run into more of the Castle clan, and then go pay Miss Mabelle a visit.

On a tip from Todd, Longarm walked several streets back from the main drag to a Mrs. Browning's boardinghouse. He got there about six-thirty, and it appeared to him that he was in time for either the second or third setting, judging by the number of men who were coming out. He entered through a long hall into two big rooms, each of which was centered by a long dining table around which a dozen men were busy in the sole pursuit of eating their fill. Here and there, harried-looking women and girls in aprons were carrying pitchers of iced tea or platters of food and rushing back and forth, trying to keep up with the demand.

Longarm spotted an empty seat and plunged for it, managing to beat out another entrant. He paid his dollar and a half to a lady who set a fresh plate in front of him, and within twenty minutes he was convinced that it was the best dollar and a half that he had ever spent on food. He ate his fill of crisp, tender, chicken-fried veal cutlets, along with fresh okra and corn and mashed potatoes and sliced tomatoes, and some of the best coffee that he had had. Finally, he had to grudgingly choose between chocolate cake and apple or coconut pie. He chose the coconut pie and was glad he did, although he figured he'd have all three before he finally left town. In gratitude for the difference between Mrs. Browning's and the hotel's fare, he left a dollar tip for whichever one of the women who'd served him cared to take it. His only regret was the Mrs. Browning's didn't serve breakfast except to those who roomed with her. Outsiders were restricted to lunch, which was served from eleven to one, and supper, which was from five until seven. He guessed that he could survive the arrangement since he had never been much of a breakfast eater anyway.

After supper, he went back to his room and sat drinking, smoking, and thinking until about nine o'clock. He fortified himself with several slugs of the good Maryland whiskey so that his mouth wouldn't be so terribly insulted by the vile stuff they peddled as whiskey in the saloons. He checked his .38 derringer to make sure that it was securely in place in his concave belt buckle, and then headed out the door to the Elite Saloon. As he left the hotel, he saw a steady stream of men heading up the stairs, and he figured that they were heading up to see Miss Mabelle Russell. He didn't figure to go see her until later in the evening when the ribbon clerks and the forty-dollar-a-month men had spent all their allowances and were out of the way.

At the Elite, he had a couple of drinks at the bar and finally sat down at a small-stakes poker game. He hated to play at such games because you couldn't use your money as a weapon. It was just a question of who drew the best cards, and that wasn't poker. Poker wasn't just a game of luck. It was a game of skill and science understood by damn few and appreciated by even fewer.

He noticed that he got quite a few looks from the other patrons of the bar. Nobody at the table that he was playing at said anything directly to him, but behind his back he heard whispered remarks like, "That's him," "That's the one over there, that broad-shouldered fella sitting in that game."

It pleased him. It meant that his plan of getting noticed was working, but whether that would lead to anything, he couldn't yet say. All he wanted to do was appear to be a man willing to engage in just about any sort of high jinks for fun or for profit.

By eleven-thirty the Castle brothers had disappointed him by not showing up, and he quit the game and made his way out of the saloon. He reckoned to have won around twenty dollars—hardly fair wages for his time considering his skill at poker.

The streets were starting to get deserted as he turned in to the hotel lobby. Also, the stairs were cleared. Apparently, most of the young bucks who'd had the bite had already spent their money and gone home. He started up the stairs.

There was a door blocking the way on the landing at the third floor. He knocked, and was admitted by a colored woman who escorted him into what she called "de pawlaw."

Inside the parlor, which was a big room created by knocking out a number of walls between bedrooms, several bored-looking young women in fairly skimpy clothes were sitting around. The decor of the place was what

Shirley Dunn would have probably called garish, including the clothes of the young ladies, who glanced at him with studied indifference.

There was a bar at the end of the room, and he sauntered over and ordered a drink of the best whiskey they had. He was pleasantly surprised to find that it was good Tennessee corn mash. He said to the bartender, a Negro in a white jacket, "I'd like to see Miss Mabelle Russell."

"Yes, sir. She be comin' out jus' any minute. You's got to wait on her 'fore you selects yore companion for the evening."

Longarm didn't bother to answer the man, but he hadn't quite finished his drink before Miss Mabelle Russell came out from a side door. She was a striking-looking woman in her mid-thirties. She had luxurious black hair that curled to her shoulders and creamy white skin that offset it nicely. She was wearing an ornate red velvet gown trimmed with white lace. Longarm thought that she had on a touch too much makeup, but he figured if she wanted to get confused with her hired help that was her business.

She came toward him, her eyes narrowing for a second and then recognition flooding her face. She said, "It's Mr. Long, isn't it?"

He gave her a slight bow. "Yes, ma'am, Miss Mabelle. It's been a couple of years since I've been here."

She said, "As I recollect, you don't need to frequent my type of establishment. The last time you were here, if I remember correctly, you were a participant in a high-stakes poker game. Are you still in the gambling business?"

"That's correct, Miss Mabelle. I'm still just a drifting gambler."

She looked him over with a critical eye. "I reckon that you're still doing pretty good. As I recall, there were some rather sad gentlemen that left my business that night. Perhaps you even took money away that might have fallen into my hands."

He said, "I'm right sorry about that, Miss Mabelle, but that's the luck of the cards."

She laughed slightly. "What can I do for you?"

He pulled a roll of bills out of his pocket and leafed off two twenties and a ten. He said, "I'd like to buy about fifty dollars of your time."

Chapter 5

Mabelle Russell looked at the money and then at him. She said, "You must be a little confused, Mr. Long. I run this game, I don't play in it."

He laughed. "I understand that, Miss Mabelle. Of course, I must add as a gentleman that if I thought that this money would buy me more than just talk, I certainly would be glad to raise the ante as high as the pot could stand."

She nodded and gave him a curtsy. "Why, thank you, sir, but I don't think that you have quite that much money."

Longarm said, "I'd like to buy about fifty dollars worth of talk."

"Talk?"

"Yes, ma'am. You got someplace quiet that we can sit down? Shouldn't take me more than fifteen minutes. I figured that if anybody knows everything that goes on around here, you'd be the one. Will fifty dollars buy me some good eyes and ears?"

She looked thoughtful for a moment and then shrugged. She reached out and took his money and said, "Come with me."

She led him into a small room, tastefully furnished, just off the main parlor. She said, "This is my sitting room. I don't let anyone else in here except, of course, special guests like you, Mr. Long. Would you like a drink?"

"Yes, ma'am. You've got some fine whiskey out there. Apparently, you've cornered the market in this town."

She laughed. "I've heard that."

She served him herself and then sat back down on a settee. Longarm was positioned across from her in a big, overstuffed wingbacked chair.

She said, "Now, what can I do for you, Mr. Long?"

Longarm said, "I'll get right to the nub of the matter, Miss Mabelle. I'm going to surprise you. I'm thinking of getting out of the gambling business and getting into something maybe a little safer. There are three things that I know about—women, cards, and horses. There ain't no money in women, except your way, and I think I would be out of place trying to handle your job. Cards have given me a fair living for a number of years, but it is getting to where there are more and more hotheads that sit down at your table and think that the six of a kind that they have in their revolver is always gonna be the best hand."

She said, "I can't envision you having trouble that you can't handle, Mr. Long."

He said, "I can handle it, but I am getting tired of it. I'm not going to see seventeen again, maybe not even twenty. I know that it surprises you, Miss Mabelle, but I think that I would like to grow old gracefully. So that kind of leaves horses. What I have in mind is a place where I could raise common stock horses, range horses, and either sell them up north where they haven't got enough sense to know what a horse is worth, or else sell them to the army. I picked San Angelo because it's a big enough place and the land is cheap around here and there is plenty of it. It's a place where I could spread myself, but I've been bothered by something that I've heard in town."

"You've heard that they've taken to shooting cavalry soldiers around here?"

"Yes, ma'am, I have. Now I'm just wondering what it's all about. Is it just some insane person, or is there a feeling in this part of the country where they don't want any outsiders? I mean, I don't want to set up around here to sell horses to the cavalry and discover that they are going to go from shooting soldiers to shooting the man who is supplying them with horses."

She looked at him. "Why have you come to me?"

"For the reason I have told you, Miss Mabelle. If anybody knows what's going on in this town, it's you. Would you dispute that?"

She smiled slightly. Even though they were several feet apart, Longarm could sense the sexual power of the woman. He remembered it from the last time he had been there. Now it was even more evident. He didn't know what she did herself. Maybe she had a boyfriend on the side. Certainly he had never heard of her having a husband.

She said, "And you think that I would have some idea who is killing these soldiers?"

"I think that you might be able to tell me if there is a climate around here that would make it unsafe for me to go into the horse business, especially the horse business where I would be selling to the army."

She got up suddenly and crossed the room to where several decanters sat on a side table. She poured an amber liquid into a wine glass. Holding it in her delicate hand, she came back to the settee. "Sherry," she said, indicating the glass. "Sometimes I think I like it too much."

Longarm gave a slight smile. "Miss Mabelle, I have a hard time envisioning you overindulging yourself in anything. You look like a mighty strong-willed woman to me."

Her eyes crinkled with a small smile. "Do I strike you as a happy woman, Mr. Long?"

"Well, you've certainly made a place for yourself. I can't imagine you're losing money on this operation but with all due respect, Miss Mabelle, it is very difficult to tell much about a person such as yourself, reserved and aloof as you are."

She took a sip of the wine. "So I seem aloof, do I? Unapproachable?"

He said, "That's the impression that I kind of get, though I don't claim any superior knowledge on the subject."

"But you, just a moment ago, said that you knew about three things. Women were one of them. Don't you consider me a woman?"

Longarm blushed in spite of himself. He said earnestly, "My Lord, yes, Miss Mabelle. I don't think that anybody in their right mind would take you for anything but a woman, and a woman of the finest kind, in all ways."

"How do you mean? Do you mean that like I think you do?"

Longarm nodded. "Indeed I do."

"So then you don't find me so unapproachable?"

Longarm said carefully, "Maybe it's just that the occasion or the circumstances haven't come up. Given the right time and the right place, I reckon that I can be induced to approach you."

She laughed. The high tinkling laugh was pleasing to the ear. She said, "Are you unapproachable, Mr. Long?"

He locked his eyes with hers. "I'll let you make a decision on that yourself, Miss Mabelle," he said, "I don't think that a woman like yourself would have much trouble approaching an old rounder like me. But we are kind of getting off the subject here. Maybe it is deliberate on your part." He narrowed his eyes at her. "Maybe you don't want to talk about this particular business."

She shrugged. "It makes me no never mind. It's just that I can't tell you anything. I don't think that there is anyone in this town who knows who is killing those soldiers except for the one who is doing it."

Longarm said, "It's not just that. It's also this attempt to get them to move the fort. I've been hearing that too, even before I got here."

She waved her free hand airily. "Oh, that. I don't think you should put too much stock in that. It's just the Castles. For some reason, they don't like this army garrison here. Maybe it's because they are bringing up stolen cattle from Mexico. I don't know. They've got the sheriff in their pocket. Maybe they're afraid the soldiers might take a hand."

Longarm was surprised to hear her talk so easily about the Castles bringing in stolen Mexican cattle, but he let it pass. He said, "It's not just that. I've heard the mayor and the city council have been writing to the War Department and the governor trying to get this garrison moved out of here. I find that hard to believe. Those soldier boys spend a lot of money in this town. I imagine that you see a lot of it in here."

She said, "It's not the mayor, Mr. Long, and it's not the council. The mayor and the council do what the Castles tell them to do, just like the sheriff. I can believe that they have their reasons as I've stated for wanting that army post moved, but I can't believe that they would be behind something so silly such as shooting the soldiers. That would just make the army dig in their heels harder and be more determined to stay. As big as the whole clan is, I don't think that the Castles believe that bushwhacking soldiers is the way to get rid of the fort."

Longarm nodded. "That would make sense, wouldn't it? No, the army would take a damned dim view of being faced down by a bushwhacker and pulling out of a long-established garrison post just because a few of their soldiers have been killed. Hell, they can print those soldiers just about as fast as they print money. There ain't never any shortage of people who can't find no other work ready to join the cavalry and go waste their lives out in the big middle of nowhere. No, I have to agree with you on that. But you do say that the Castles are pushing for the garrison to leave. Do you have any idea why, besides this business of the stolen cattle?"

She shrugged her shoulders again. "No, and I don't really know why they should be so concerned about the army. Hell, the army's not interested in who's bringing in stolen cattle. Supposedly, they are here to defend us from the Indians. The nearest one of which I think is about five hundred miles from here."

Longarm finished his drink in a quick move. He said, "Well, it's certainly got me puzzled. But I appreciate your time, Miss Mabelle."

She held out her hand to him. The fifty dollars was in it. She said, "Here. Take this."

He was about to get up but he settled back down. "Why would I want to take that back?"

"I didn't do you any good. One of the rules of this house is that if you don't satisfy the customer, he doesn't have to pay. I didn't give you any answers that could have possibly satisfied you."

Longarm said, "Ma'am, I said that I would pay fifty dollars for a few minutes of your time. I didn't say that I had to get satisfaction out of it. No, a deal is a deal. That's your money."

She thrust the bills at him. "Do me a favor and take it. I don't want any money hanging between us."

He slowly began to understand what she was talking about. He asked, "Am I hearing what I think I am hearing?"

She said, "Tomorrow night is Wednesday night. We close on Wednesdays. Would you come have dinner with me here?"

He said, "Well, I'd be right honored, Miss Mabelle."

"Then take this money and cut out the Miss Mabelle la-ti-da. You and I are a lot alike, Custis. We may wear the clothes but underneath, we are a couple of rounders. Now take the money."

He reluctantly accepted the fifty dollars from her and said, "What time shall I come for dinner?"

"About seven. Do you want another drink?"

He stood up slowly. "No, it's late. I thank you very much, though. I am looking forward to tomorrow night. I'm gonna get up early in the morning and do some scouting around and look over some property. I guess I'd best get on back to my hotel . . . actually, I am in my hotel, so I guess I'll get on back to the first floor and get some sleep."

She came around the table and offered him her hand. He took it and gave it a light kiss. Before he could realize what was happening, she was in his arms and their lips were meeting. It was a brief kiss but it sent tingles all through Longarm. He backed toward the door.

He said, "I'll be looking forward to tomorrow night."

She said, "Yes, good night, Custis."

He left Mabelle Russell and went down to his room a great deal more enlightened and a good deal more mystified than when he'd gone up. Now the finger seemed to point directly at the Castles. What had previously been thought to be a widespread interest in having the army garrison removed now came down to the interest of just one family. Though for the life of him, he couldn't see how the army would be any threat to the Castles, even if they were bringing in Mexican cattle, stolen or otherwise. For many years it had been a dodge in that barren country to bring in Mexican cattle, especially if you were fairly close to the border, to supplement your herd.

What a big cattleman did was to bring in a buyer from one of the large cattle-buying outfits in St. Louis or Kansas City or Abilene and show them his regular stock. The buyer would pay sixty-five or seventy or maybe even eighty dollars a head for a thousand head or five hundred head, and then he would go on back to the city to await delivery. Then the cattleman would mix in a couple hundred of the Mexican steers, which were worth about twenty or twenty-five dollars apiece, and make an extra profit on the business without ever having done much more than obtaining the cattle and taking them on the short drive to his ranch. Of course, there was the matter of the branding. But since they didn't brand cattle in Mexico, his brand would be the only one on the cow.

It was enlightening to know that it was the Castles who were putting the pressure on the garrison to move, but as Mabelle Russell had said, she didn't see where the Castles would be dumb enough to think that murdering a few soldiers was going to get the army to move the fort. He didn't think so either. In fact, it would have exactly the opposite effect.

What had him mystified was the sudden way she had taken to him. He hadn't done much more than say hello before she'd started putting out ripples like a stone dropped in a still lake. He had felt her, he had smelled her, he had seen her, and she had given him back his money. Mabelle Russell didn't seem the type to give back anyone's money for any reason. And now he was invited to dinner.

He got undressed, put his revolver ready to hand on the nightstand, and got into bed full of questions, but as was his habit, he put them out of his mind. They couldn't be answered that night and all they could do would be to interfere with his sleep. He had one last drink, then turned down the bedside lamp until it flickered and the room grew dark. His last thought as he went to sleep was the amazing contrast between the delicate, dainty, and exquisite Mrs. Shirley Dunn and the robust, hardy, sexual excitement of Mabelle Russell.

Chapter 6

He awoke the next morning to the news that there had been another murder. He heard it from his waitress in the hotel dining room while he was having breakfast. She said it offhandedly as if she expected that he already knew. He had been about to put a biscuit in his mouth when he dropped it to the table and stared at her.

He said, "What?"

She said, "Aw, yeah. They killed another one of those soldier boys last night. Somebody found him this morning coming into town. I figured that you already knew. It's the talk of the town."

He said, "Where was he found?"

She shrugged. "Oh, I don't know. I think it was on that road out of town that leads to Fort Concho. It might have been someplace else. I really didn't pay much attention to it."

He hurried through his breakfast as fast as he could, and then went back to his room to deliberate. He needed information and he needed it badly while the murder was still fresh. He doubted the wisdom of going to the sheriff, who would most certainly know but would be most certainly interested in Longarm's curiosity. He could pick up information from the men on the street or in the saloons, but that would be unreliable and perhaps distorted. In the end, he decided that it was worth a visit to the fort to get as many fresh details as he could, even if some people began to wonder why he found it so necessary to visit the garrison commander so often.

Just as he was finishing his deliberations, Todd came in to give him the news. When Longarm assured him that he had already heard, the boy said, "Kind of a shame, ain't it, Mr. Long?"

Longarm said, "Oh, I don't know. They ain't doin' much good around here. Who was it that got killed anyhow?"

"I heard that it was one of them officers, you know, one of them high-ranking kinds. Not like the ones that they've been killing before but one of them . . . you know, the ones that gives the orders?"

Longarm nodded. If that was the case, then indeed the case had turned serious. Killing some farm boy from Iowa who had enlisted to get off the farm was one thing, but killing an officer who most likely was from some influential family was another. Whoever was doing the killings had now upped the ante. He had also shown some knowledge of the military.

Longarm told Todd to saddle his bay mare and bring it around to the front of the hotel, saying that he would be along shortly. The young man nodded, hesitated a second, and then finally started toward the door. He stopped and turned and said, "Mr. Long, can I ask you something?"

Longarm nodded. "Well, if it don't cost money or scare the horses. What?"

Todd fidgeted for a moment. "Well, this is a kind of delicate proposition, you understand, Mr. Long. What I was wondering, if a man was to find an army horse just running loose out on the prairie when that man was comin' in to work early in the morning . . . well, if'n he found that horse, that horse wouldn't be his, would it, Mr. Long?"

"He found the horse of the officer that was shot?"

Todd said hastily, "No, sir! I ain't saying that. I'm just saying that I found a saddled and bridled army horse that was running loose. In case that you ain't knowed about it, that's the first one of the horses of the men that have been shot that's ever been found and I'm the one that found it. You understand what I am saying, Mr. Long?"

Longarm nodded slowly. It was a fact that he had overlooked. He said, "Are you telling me that of the soldiers that were shot, none of their horses were never recovered?"

Todd nodded. "Yes, sir. That's what I'm a-saying. Of course, I ain't talking about that one that was stabbed in the back alley. He was just walking. He wasn't a-horseback."

"Where have you got this horse?"

Todd looked down at the floor. "Am I gonna get in trouble about this?"

"Not if you tell the truth."

"I taken him to my cousin's barn on the outside of town. I unsaddled him, unbridled him, and gave him a bait of oats and gave him some water. He was spooked, sure as hell."

Longarm said, "The smell of blood spooks horses, Todd."

"Well, what am I supposed to do now?"

"One thing that you're supposed to do is not to tell anyone else, do you hear me?"

Longarm reached in his pocket and found a five-dollar gold piece. He flipped it across the space between them. He said, "Do you understand me when I say that you are not to tell anyone else?"

Todd looked surprised at the coin he had caught in the air. This was probably the first time he'd had five dollars all together at any one time in his life.

He said, "Yes, sir, Mr. Long. I am gonna do exactly what you tell me. *Prexactly!*"

"Then just leave that horse where he is. Scurry on around and bring me my horse, and then this afternoon I want you to show me *that* horse. Do you understand?"

"Yes, sir! I'm tending to it right now. I'm already saddling your horse."

Longarm waited until he was gone and then he had a double pull off the rapidly diminishing bottle of Maryland whiskey that he had opened the day before. After that, he got up, stretched, and checked his revolver. He put on his hat and started for the front of the hotel. He didn't think it would take Todd very long to have his horse ready.

Todd was waiting for him as he stepped off the porch and into the street. Just before he swung into the saddle, Longarm looked around at the young boy and said, "Todd, is there anybody around here that goes way back and could give me a feel of this place? I mean, I'm a man who when he is thinking of going into business in a particular area wants to know everything he can about it. I'm a man who believes in being thorough. So, do you know of anybody who has been around here steady for a good number of years who would have a pretty good idea of the people

81

and the history and where all the bodies are buried and that sort of thing?"

The open face of the sandy-haired young man screwed up for a moment while he thought about it. "Well, there's ol' Clell Martin."

"Who is he?"

Todd said, "Well, he's . . . I don't know. He's just an old gentleman been in and around here since anybody can remember. I think he was born here or something."

Longarm said, "Where would I find him?"

Todd made a vague gesture toward the northeast. "Well, he's got an old place, little-bitty old place, off up yonder about halfway to the fort. It's back off that main road a good two miles to the north. I tell you, Mr. Long, I ain't too sure that he'd be the right one to talk to, though."

"Why not?"

"Well, he's a little strange."

"What do you mean, strange?"

Todd said, "Well, the story is at one time he used to be a Texas Ranger. Not for very long 'cause they say he took a bullet in the head. It didn't kill him, but they say he's still carrying it. I guess it was in the Texas Rangers that he got that. I don't know, they tell so many stories about old Clell Martin that it is hard to keep up with him, but he has some pretty strong opinions about stuff. But if there's anybody that knows the country and knows the people around here and such, it would be him."

"What about the Castles? Don't they go back a pretty good ways?

Todd looked surprised. "Hell, the Castles? Mr. Long, the Castles ain't been here as long as I've been alive. They're from Kentucky or some such place up in there. They ain't native to this part of the country."

Longarm nodded. "Clell Martin, huh? Much obliged, Todd." He swung aboard the bay mare and pointed her out of town toward the fort. Clell Martin sounded interesting, but not enough to be in a hurry about seeing him. As Longarm cleared the town, he put the mare into a lope to cover the few miles to the fort.

Captain Montrose was behind his desk looking grim-faced when Longarm was shown into his office. With a curt nod of his head, the commander indicated a chair for Longarm to sit in.

The first words out of his mouth were, "Well, now they have commenced killing officers."

Longarm said, "So I've heard. Who was it?"

"A young second lieutenant named Singleton. He'd only been posted out here about a month. Twenty-five years old, graduate of the Virginia Military Institute, and a very promising young officer. I cannot believe this. I cannot believe that such despicable actions could take place within the confines of the United States of America."

Longarm thought for a moment. "Does anybody have any idea what time the lieutenant might have been shot?"

Captain Montrose said, "The best that we can figure, it must have been close to midnight. He had struck up a friendship with a young lady in town and he was with her and her parents until a few minutes after eleven. Figure about ten or fifteen minutes for a good-bye to her, figure coming from the other side of town hitting the road to the fort and the time it took him to travel the four miles that he had traveled judging from where he was found this morning, and you come up with about midnight. He was less than a mile from the fort when some no-good, low-down sonofabitch struck him down."

Longarm said, "Have you got the body here?"

"Yes, sir. We've got him in the ice house. We are waiting for instructions from his family as to what to do with the body. I am sure they would want him shipped back home to be buried there."

"Was he shot more than once?"

"Hell, Marshal. If you could see the size of the hole in him, you'd realize that one shot was all that was needed."

With Captain Montrose leading, they left his office and went beyond the buildings that bordered the quadrangle to a stone and log building set off by itself at the back of the fort. It was small and compact with a flat roof.

The captain worked the door to open it and they stepped inside. It took a moment for the captain to light the kerosene lamp so that they could see. By its illumination, Longarm was able to see the body of the young officer still in uniform laid out on the table in the middle of the room. All around the walls were big cakes of ice and toward the back, hanging on hooks, were sides of beef, pork, and goats. Together they stepped over to the body and looked down at the young man. In death, he looked even younger than twenty-five years old. On the front of his jacket-blouse was a large angry red stain.

Longarm said, "I want to see where the bullet entered."

With Captain Montrose's help, he turned over the body, now rigid with rigor mortis. The young man had been shot just to the right of the left shoulder blade. It had made a neat, almost round hole as it had entered. Longarm calculated it would have exactly pierced the young man's heart on the way through his body, killing him instantly.

As they laid the body down on its back, Longarm said, "Well, at least he never knew what hit him."

"The sonofabitch," the captain said, "or the sonofabitches—whoever pulled the damn trigger."

Longarm said, "Let's open his blouse, Captain. I want to see if we can figure out what he got shot with."

Together they unbuttoned the young man's tunic. It seemed to Longarm that Captain Montrose shuddered a little as he performed the unpleasant task. They pulled the blouse back and then the shirt. There was a gaping wound on the left side of the young man's chest.

"My God," the captain said. "You can put your fist in there."

Longarm said thoughtfully, "Well, it's a damn cinch that he wasn't shot with no carbine. That's a soft-nosed bullet, not copper-clad."

Captain Montrose said, "Would a .44 make that size hole?"

Longarm shook his head. "No, that looks like a Sharps to me. A .50-caliber Sharps buffalo gun. I ain't seen that big of an exit hole in a long time." He looked a moment more and then started buttoning the young man's clothes. He looked up at the face and said, "Young and innocent and stiff and dead. It's a damn shame. Let's go back to your office and talk about this."

There really wasn't much to talk about. Captain Montrose wanted to know what Longarm was going to do, and Longarm couldn't tell him because Longarm didn't know. He said, "Captain, this is a hell of a big country. There are thousands of places where a bushwhacker could lay in wait and at the time they are doing the killing, there is nobody around to see. Can't you keep your men on post for the time being?"

Captain Montrose said helplessly, "I can't expect these men after their rigorous duties in the field to sit here just five miles from entertainment. Marshal, you have no idea how dreary, how wearisome barracks life is for the common soldier." The captain shook his head. "I never had any idea they would kill an officer."

"I thought that was the ones they went for first."

Captain Montrose glanced over at him. "That's in battle. This is not a battle. This is murder. In battle, you try to take out the other side's leaders. This was just a young boy returning from a social engagement before some cowardly sonofabitch shot him in the back."

Longarm said, "It appeared to me that the angle of the bullet was downward. It looked to me that somebody was on higher ground than the lieutenant was. That ball went in by his shoulder blade and came out near his bottom rib, though it was hard to tell as messed up as it was." He was thoughtful for a moment. "If it was a Sharps, it has a hell of a carrying range, four or five hundred yards, but at night, that would take a hell of a shot, especially at a man on a moving horse."

Longarm got up and continued. "Captain, I may have to take some drastic action." He told the captain what he had heard about the Castle family. "I don't know what is causing them to covet your place so bad, but it may be that they want it bad enough to kill your troops. I can't think of any other reason, can you?"

Captain Montrose shook his head. "No, I can't. But if I thought that it was the Castles, I would take a company of men to each of their ranches, burn their damn places down, kill all of their stock, and then hang them. The face of that young officer is going to be with me for the rest of my life. And what do I write and tell his parents? That he was killed in action while returning from a visit to his girl-friend? Shot by a cowardly, west Texas bushwhacker?"

Longarm said, "I know you are bitter, Captain, and I know you are angry, but that ain't gonna get us no nearer to the killer. I may have to put on this badge and start arresting some folks to get some answers."

Captain Montrose looked at him and said, "Maybe if you had done that in the first place, this young man wouldn't be dead."

Longarm gave him a sharp look. "Captain, one badge can't be but in one place at a time, and whoever is insane enough to kill five soldiers is not going to stop at killing the sixth just because there is a U.S. marshal around. There is plenty of law around here. There is a sheriff with two deputies. There is a town marshal. That hasn't stopped them. What makes you think that my badge would?"

The captain looked down at his desk. He said, "I'm sorry. I didn't mean it."

Longarm nodded. "I understand." He put on his hat. "I better get back to town. I've got some thinking to do."

It was a fine morning as he let the mare ease her way back to town. About two miles from the fort, he noticed a path leading off to the right. In the distance, he could barely make out a shack of some kind made noticeable only by a thin trail of smoke coming from a cooking fire. The shack itself was so weathered that it blended in with the dead grays and browns of the countryside. He thought that it was most likely Clell Martin's place. It was just about where Todd had told him it would be.

With not much of an idea of what he waⁱ going to find out or even what he was going to say, he turned the mare on the trail and spurred her into a lope. He went a good mile and a half or two miles back into the rough prairie land. As he covered the distance, he noticed that just to his right were a pair of twin buttes rising perhaps five hundred feet in the air. They were about a half a mile from the main road he had just left. As he passed them, the thought stuck him that such a place might be an ideal station for a sharpshooting bushwhacker. Perhaps Mr. Martin had heard the sound of a gunshot. Perhaps he had seen men moving about at night. Sometimes old men didn't sleep too soundly. He knew that in the latter years of his life his grandfather had slept only two or three hours a night.

A quarter of a mile from the weather-beaten shack, he pulled his horse down to a trot and then a walk. It didn't do to come upon these old nesters too suddenly. They had a way of shooting strangers first and then discussing it with the sheriff later. Behind the house was a fair-sized barn and then two other outbuildings and several corrals. He could see a few mules and a few milk cows and some steers held up close to the place, obviously being grain-fed and perhaps supplied with hay. It surprised him. It was a much more prosperous operation than he would have expected. He had even heard a rooster crow and knew that the old man had chickens, which actually wasn't all that surprising since nearly everyone out in the country kept chickens since they were cheap to buy and cheap to keep up. Fresh eggs were a treat. When he was within fifty yards of the ranch house, he began calling out loud, "Hello!" On the third hail, he saw the front door of the cabin open and a small, thin, stooped man came out and stand on the rickety front porch. Longarm rode on up, still without any idea what he was going to say.

He pulled his horse to a stop a few yards from the porch. The old man shuffled forward a step or two. Longarm said, "Hidee." He made no move to dismount. You didn't get down unless you were asked.

The old man was looking at him suspiciously. He said, "Yes, and what would you be a-wantin'."

Longarm said, "Actually, I don't want anything. I was just looking the countryside over and spied your place and thought I'd stop and talk a minute."

The old man was still looking at him suspiciously. He said, "You ain't come out with no papers of any kind from those damn Castles, have you?"

Longarm smiled. Without half thinking about it, he had an idea that the old man was squatting on the property and the Castles were trying to incorporate it into their domain. He said, "No, I can assure you that I ain't no friend of the Castles. In fact, I had quite a run-in with that young bull, Billy Bob, in the saloon the other night."

Some of the suspicion cleared from the old man's face. He said, "You . . . you mean that you had it out with old Billy Bob? You don't look dead." He cackled.

Longarm said, "Well, I cracked him over the head with the barrel of my revolver before he could get close enough to get those arms around me. After about four or five of those licks, Mr. Martin, he didn't want to wrestle no more."

The old man cackled again and slapped his thigh. He said, "Good for you. Good for you." Then a curtain seemed to drop over his face. "How do you know my name?"

"I was out at the fort and I had noticed this place going to it. I asked them who lived here and they told me. No mystery about it, Mr. Martin."

The suspicion on the old man's face was stronger than ever. He said, "You were out to the fort, hanging around them soldier boys?"

Longarm said, "Well, the fact of the matter is I had an invoice against the United States Cavalry for some horses

I had sold them, and I either want my horses back or I want my money. Part of them horses are here at this fort. I came here trying to get justice. So far, I haven't got it. That's what I am doing in this country. I do like this country and I've been thinking about locating a little ranch here."

The old man nodded slowly. He said, "So them blue-coats ain't been doing you right?"

Longarm said, "Well, if you consider stealing a man's property and his money doing him right, then they've been doing real right with me. I've been to Fort Mason, Fort Stockton, and now here. I've found my horses at every one of them. I've got this warrant from the Quartermaster Corps to be paid for seventy-five head of horses and I ain't seen a penny, so I don't really calculate that as being right."

The old man spat into the dust off the edge of the porch. He said, "Why don't you step on down off of your horse and come on in and drink a cup of coffee with me?"

Longarm said, "Well, that would be mighty hospitable of you. I'd like that."

He swung his leg over, dismounted, and dropped the reins knowing that his bay mare would ground-rein and impress the old man. He said, "But more than the coffee, I would be mighty obliged to a man who I reckon would know this country about as well as anybody."

Clell Martin said, "Well, man and boy, pushing fifty years. I've been around here just about as close as a man can stick. I went off to a war and went off to some foolishness with the Texas Rangers, but other than that, I've been pretty well right around here close at hand."

Longarm stepped up onto the porch and followed the old man through the door and into the house. He noticed that Clell Martin sort of dragged a leg as he walked. He said, "I see you've got a bum leg there, Mr. Martin. Anything sudden, or does that go back a ways?" They were turning left out of the tiny sitting room into a cluttered kitchen.

Martin said, "Sit yourself down there at the kitchen table. I'll hot this coffee up and we'll have a cup." While he busied himself with the coffeepot and some tin cups, the old man said, "I caught a ball in the hip about twenty years ago. It's plagued me ever since. Some days are worse than others."

Longarm said, "Depends on the weather, I take it?"

"Yeah, though sometimes lately it seems like it's nearly all the time."

Longarm was looking around the cluttered room. He could tell that it hadn't had a woman's touch in many a year. He said, "Heard tell that you were with the Texas Rangers, Mr. Martin."

At the stove, the old man shrugged his shoulders. "Well, not so's that you could notice. Was right after the Confederacy. Them Yankee carpetbaggers that came down here talking about Reconstruction made out that they were reforming the Texas Rangers, but it was just a bunch of hoorah. Turned out that they just wanted us to do their dirty deeds for them. I got a bullet between my scalp and my skull for my troubles. I wasn't with them more than six months. I came on back here and tried to scratch what living I could out of dry dirt and scrawny cattle."

"You running any cattle now?"

"Oh, I have about a hundred head. They're scattered all over."

Longarm said, "Well, it's as good a time a year to have your cattle out. I guess what water there is, they'll find."

Martin said disgustedly, "Yeah, what water there is. Them damn Castles got most of the water, and naturally them damn soldier boys got what's left."

He poured up two steaming cups of coffee out of a tin pot and brought them on over to the table. He set one in front of Longarm and then eased himself into a chair, wincing slightly with his hip.

Longarm said, "You don't care much for them Castles, do you?"

"Well, if you care for highfalutin, smart-aleck, stingy neighbors who try to take a man's property, I guess you could say that I care about them. About the same way you care about them thieving army boys. How come they won't give you your money for those horses?"

Longarm said, "I don't know. Some kind of paperwork. Seems like it's all confused. I go to one quartermaster and he says I have the wrong set of papers, that I have got to go to some other place to get the other set of papers. All I know is that I delivered seventy-five horses, I got a bill of sale for them, but I don't have no damn money for them. I came down to get either my horses or my money. But I ain't having much luck."

The old man smiled knowingly. "That's those damned bluecoats for ya. They ain't worth a damn. Half of them are fer'ners, you know, they don't even come from this country. Can you imagine anything worse than a Yankee fer'ner? Ha!"

Longarm looked at him for a second. He said, "What outfit were you with, Mr. Martin?"

Old Man Martin seemed to grow a foot in his chair as he said proudly, "I was with Hood's brigade. The A-number-one outfit out of Texas. I was a sergeant, by golly, and damn proud of it. There is a few of them blue bellies pushing up daisies, tried to cross that Red River and didn't quite make it. Yes, sir. I was very proud to be a member of Hood's brigade."

A thought was growing in Longarm's mind but it needed time to develop. He said, "The Castles are trying to push you off this land, aren't they?"

The old man looked up in surprise. "How did you know that?"

"Well, Mr. Martin, part of the job of being a horse trader is being able to see things in folks. I have a feeling that you ain't got clear title to this property, and it ain't as if the Castles ain't got enough, but they are trying to push you off what little bit you've got."

Clell Martin slammed his hand down the kitchen table hard enough to make the dishes rattle. He said, "There, by God, sir. You have the bite of it. That's the truth and the facts. Them low-down, no-good sonofabitches. Yes, sir, trying to push an old man off his property. A man who fought for his country, a man who took a ball for his country, a man that was even in the service of the state."

Longarm said, "You know, I'd like to play a dirty trick on the Castles. Would there be any chance that you'd help me?"

The old man's face lit up. "You just say the word. I'm there."

Longarm said casually, "You wouldn't happen to have a long-range rifle, would you by any chance? High-caliber?"

Clell Martin said, "Ha! You wouldn't believe it, but I still have my Springfield from the War of the Confederacy. You know, of course, we didn't have no proper arms like the Yankees did, so I took me one of them modern

Springfield breechloaders off one of them blue bellies. Still got it. Fires a .58-caliber cartridge."

Longarm said, "That might come in handy." He sipped at his coffee, watching the old man over the rim. They talked for another half hour, and Longarm managed to make his way through two of the bitterest cups of coffee that he had ever tasted. Finally, when he felt that his visit was as fruitful as it was going to get, he made his adieus with a promise to come back and discuss their mutual problem at greater length. After he had mounted, he said, "Mr. Martin, I think you and I are going to do some business. I consider you, sir, a citizen and a patriot."

The old man seemed to straighten up. He said, "I like to think of myself that way."

"Well, we need more like you. I'm going into town now and do some thinking and some planning. I'll be on out here. It just might be that we can help each other."

Clell Martin said, "Well, that would just suit me jam up to. jelly."

Longarm rode away in a very thoughtful frame of mind. That the old man had an old Civil War Springfield did not surprise him. They had been manufactured toward the end of the war by the Union forces in the hundreds of thousands. There were probably a many a one hanging over fireplaces or stored in attics all over the country. Of course, in the years since, they had been replaced by the all-metallic cartridge rather than the cap-and-ball mechanism that had operated the Springfield. The old rifles were slow but they were extremely effective. However, they were not the only long-range rifle that fired a large-caliber slug. Any number of buffalo guns, most notably the Sharps, did the same.

But he found it most interesting that Clell Martin had such a hate for the Castles. At one part of the conversation, Longarm had wondered out loud what effect it would have on the peace and tranquility of the Castle family if they both got up on top of one of the buttes near one of the Castle ranch headquarters and lobbed a few shells though the ranch house roof. The old man had cackled with glee at the very thought.

But there was still a question that Longarm wanted answered. The best man for that was one of the town's undertakers. He assumed that it would have had to have been an undertaker who'd readied the bodies of the soldiers to be shipped back home for their burial. However, only part of his mind was dwelling on the subject of the murdered soldiers. Other parts of it were playing around with the delightful prospect of dinner with the delicious Miss Mabelle Russell that evening. It was the one bright spot in an otherwise dreary time. As he rode toward town, he couldn't keep from wondering where Billy Bob and his brother Glenn had been the night before. The deputy had warned him that they would come looking for him, but they hadn't. What business could have been so important to keep them from seeking revenge? His problem was that he had no way of finding out. He simply couldn't go around asking questions and he couldn't go to the sheriff. He'd didn't know any way to get any information without putting on his badge, and he wasn't ready to do that.

Yet.

When he got into town he inquired about undertakers, and was surprised to find that there was only one. With the state of civility in a place like San Angelo, he'd figured that they would need at least a half a dozen. He got directions and rode to the other side of town and pulled up in front of the building. As he dismounted from his mare, he noticed that there was a barbershop right next door, and it reminded him that it might be a good idea to get a haircut and a store-bought shave before his dinner that evening with Miss Russell.

Longarm learned very little from the undertaker, though the man was willing enough. He was an affable, plump man named Charlie something—Longarm never did get his last name. The undertaker had handled all of the bodies, including the one that had been stabbed. He had a vivid memory of each one. In fact, he went out of his way to make it clear to Longarm that he took pride in his work and in his handling of the bodies that were in his care. Of all the soldiers who had been shot, only one body had seemed to indicate that the bullet had been fired from an elevated position. Charlie was quick, and as soon as he caught on to what Longarm was after, he was able to draw on a piece of paper the locations of the entrance and exit wounds of all the soldiers who had been shot. One shot had been shot from a level position, which meant that the assassin must have been standing or kneeling or in concealment on a slight rise. The other two entrance wounds had been lower than the exit wounds. In all cases, however, it was clear that a high-powered, long-range rifle of a high caliber had been used since the exit wound had been so much larger than the entry.

The result was that Longarm had left the undertaker no wiser than when he had entered. He was not at all surprised that each of the murders had been committed with a long-range, high-caliber rifle. That only made sense. If you were going to ambush a man, it made sense to do it from as far a distance as possible, and that meant a long-range rifle. If you wanted to make sure that you killed him, that meant a heavy-caliber slug. But the information was virtually useless since he had no idea of how many old Springfields like Clell Martin owned or how many Sharps buffalo rifles or other high-powered long-range heavy-caliber rifles there were in the county. They probably numbered in the fifties or the hundreds. He doubted that he would find his killer through the weapon. His visit to the undertaker had been in the hope that all of the ambushing had been done from an elevated height, which would indicate that someone was using a position on one of the buttes, and that could point in the direction of Clell Martin. But he really couldn't suspect Clell Martin because he didn't have a solid reason. The Castles continued to be foremost in his mind only for the flimsy reason that he had no one better. And also because Billy Bob and Glenn had not come looking for him last night the last trooper had been killed, and because the Castles were behind the effort to move the fort.

It was in a thoughtful mood that he went into the barbershop to get a haircut and a shave. It was a three-chair barbershop and there were quite a number of loungers hanging around. After the barber finished trimming Longarm's hair, he leaned the chair back so that Longarm was lying almost horizontally and began lathering his face for the shave. As he lay there with the barber putting hot towels on to soften his bristly whiskers, he chanced to hear a couple of the loafers laughing about Virgil Castle. He just caught the end of the remark, which sounded like, "... and you know that they found that fool running nekkid down the road with a rifle in his hand ..." Another voice chimed in to say, "Yeah, I heard about that. You know that the boy gets stranger and stranger every year."

Longarm suddenly got very curious. He asked the barber, "Who are they talking about?"

The barber was stropping his razor. He turned to Longarm and said, "Oh, one of Vernon Castle's sons. He ain't quite right, a little strange."

Longarm said, "They called him a boy? Is he young?"

The barber answered, "Naw, he's about twenty-five. He just ain't ever growed up."

"Is he dangerous?"

"Naw, he just . . . he just ain't quite right. That's about all you can say about him."

Longarm said, "When was he found wandering down the road with a rifle?"

The barber was busy scraping away at Longarm's face. He stopped and wiped the razor on the cloth under Longarm's chin, then asked, "What would be your interest, mister? You a friend of the Castles? You must not be or you'd know who Virgil is."

Longarm said, "Well, just general interest. I'm a . . . new in town. If there is someone running around naked carrying a rifle, I guess I'd just kind of like to know about that."

He said, "The Castles are highly regarded around here. We don't do much talking about them."

Longarm asked, "Well, by any chance was it last night that he was found wandering down the road?"

The barber didn't bother to stop shaving Longarm's face. To Longarm, it seemed like he dug the razor in a little deeper. The barber said, "Like I said, mister, the Castles are pretty highly regarded hereabouts. We don't do much talking about them. It ain't good for business, if you know what I mean."

"Suit yourself. Really ain't none of my business anyways. I'll be riding on in a couple of days."

"That might not be a bad idea."

When the barber was finished, Longarm got out of the chair and paid for the shave and the haircut. He put his hat on and carefully looked at the two loafers he had heard talking before walking outside. He stood on the boardwalk for a moment thinking, then as if on sudden impulse, mounted his horse and set off at a good pace for the railroad station and the telegraph office.

What he was going to do was a long shot and not particularly legal. Technically, the action that he was about to take was within his jurisdiction, but it was not the sort of thing that Billy Vail would smile about.

Once at the telegrapher's office, he wrote out his message, took it over to the operator, and handed it to him silently. He watched the man's face as he read it. When the man had finished the rather long message, he looked up, startled, at Longarm.

Longarm said evenly, "I'm going to give you some advice, my friend. That message is federal government business. If it goes out of this office . . . if any word of it comes out of your mouth, even to your grandmother, there is an outstanding chance that you'll be spending a pretty good chunk of your life at Leavenworth Prison."

The telegraph operator, who was a thin, chalky man with sunken cheeks, stared at him and gulped. Longarm slowly pulled his badge out and, holding it in the palm of his hand, shoved it in front of the telegrapher's face.

He said, "Take a good look at it. Don't make any mistakes."

The telegrapher finally found his voice. He said, "Yes, sir. Yes, sir. I ain't saying a word. Yes, sir. No, sir."

Longarm said, "I just don't want you to get confused as to who carries the most weight, the Castles or the United States government. In a fair fight, the United States government is going to win every time."

"Yes, sir!" the telegrapher said.

"Send it."

"Yes, sir." The telegrapher wheeled on his stool, went to his desk, and began hitting the wireless key.

Longarm listened to the dots and dashes, knowing what the message said. He had wired a friend of his, a deputy marshal in Omaha, Nebraska. He had asked the deputy marshal to find a friendly federal judge and have that judge wire him a warrant for the arrest of the Castle family for the illegal importation of Mexican cattle and the illegal sale of those cattle inside the United States. He had closed the telegram by asking his friend not to question the reason, saying that he was on the track of something far more serious than the movement of Mexican cattle, and that he needed a handhold somewhere so he could move some of the obstacles that were blocking his path. He was fairly certain that his friend would understand and comply. He had chosen Omaha instead of Kansas City or St. Louis because he was fairly certain that the Castles would ship cattle to Omaha and the deputy marshal in Omaha happened to be a good friend of his. It was as simple as that.

When the message was sent, the telegrapher looked expectantly at Longarm as if awaiting further instructions. Longarm disappointed him by simply paying for the telegram and leaving without another word. He took the blank on which he had written out the message with him.

He rode back to his hotel, had a late lunch at a little cafe just down the street from the Cutler, and then went to his room, poured himself a drink, and sat down on the bed to think.

He was almighty curious about Virgil Castle. Could the killings indeed be the work of a weak-minded member of a powerful clan? Maybe they were too smart to believe that they could move the army by killing individual soldiers, but perhaps Virgil was a little too thickheaded to understand that and had just been trying to help matters along in his own muddled way. It made a plausible explanation. The man could have overheard his father or his brothers talking about the garrison, saying that it was standing in their way, and figured that the simplest way would be to shoot a soldier. He still didn't know when Virgil had been spotted naked carrying a rifle, or even which road he had been seen on. Longarm immediately set his glass aside and went in search of Todd.

He found the young man in the lobby of the hotel. He drew him aside, told him what he had heard in the barbershop, and asked Todd if he had heard the same.

Todd looked around nervously. "Mr. Long, I don't reckon that we ought to be talking about the Castles, especially Virgil. They don't allow nobody to make fun of him."

Longarm said, "I just want to know when he was seen walking naked down a road carrying a rifle."

Todd looked around again to make sure that no one could overhear him. "It was last night . . . late last night."

"You mean, like midnight or after?"

"Yes, sir," Todd said. Then, with an appeal in his voice, he said, "Mr. Long, you ain't gonna tell nobody that I told ya, are you?"

Longarm gave him an impatient look. "Todd, I thought you and I had a deal. We don't talk about our business with anybody else. Isn't that right?"

"Yes, sir."

Longarm asked, "Do you know which road?"

For a moment Todd appeared to think the question over, then slowly shook his head. "No, sir. You see, it's mostly just gossip that gets to me. There ain't all that many particulars to it. I just kind of heard it when I was out around the stables. Things like that get started at one end of this town, and they get all changed around by the time they get to the other. Do you know what I mean?"

Longarm said, "Yes, I do." He gave Todd a silver dollar and then went back to his room, his mind turning the matter over and over. The more he thought about it, the more he liked it. Now all he needed was a little leverage to get hold of the Castles by the short hairs. A handle, a come-along.

He would have it if his friend was able to get him the bench warrant from the federal judge. That would give him the authority to arrest the Castles, to search them, to search their premises, to scare the living hell out of them.

But all that could wait. For the moment, he could allow his mind the luxury of thinking about the evening ahead with Mabelle Russell. The widow Shirley Dunn had built a fire in him with her very unusual supper. The fire was still banked and only waiting for the slightest opportunity to ignite into full blaze.

He went to his rooms and immediately set about taking a bath and slicking himself up for the engagement that grew nearer by the moment. For the time being, the law business would wait.

Chapter 7

Longarm almost dropped his fork when Mabelle Russell said almost casually halfway through supper, "When are you going to put on your badge, Marshal?"

He stared at her, trying to think of something to say. After a moment, he tried to put a lying face on. He said, "What are you talking about? Marshal? Badge? I am a gambler and a horse trader. What's this marshal stuff?"

She laughed gaily. "Oh, for God's sake, cut it out. I know who you are. When you were here three years ago you were spotted. Someone told me that you were passing yourself off then as a gambler, but you were actually the famous Marshal Custis Long, known far and wide as Longarm. I don't see where you have the gall to travel around incognito as well known as you are."

He could do no more than stare at her. Finally he said, "Mabelle, does anybody else know about this?"

She shrugged. "I doubt it."

"Then how come you know?"

She gave him a slight smile. "Don't you think that I make it my business to know every man's business who comes into my place? Do you think that I would last long in this business if I didn't have a very inquiring nature? I don't just let anybody come in here. They've got to have some sort of a recommendation. You take a small town and there will be two people that know everybody and what's going on. One of them will be the madam of the local whorehouse."

Longarm looked at her. "Who will the other one be?"

Mabelle laughed again. "Well, naturally it will be the one that the madam is paying to get her information."

Longarm laughed ruefully. "I reckon that it makes a little sense. I'm going to ask you a favor. Do you think that you can keep this under your hat for a few days? Do you reckon that you can help me out a little bit there?"

She shrugged. "I don't see why not. It makes no never mind to me, one way or the other, who's killing those soldiers. In fact, I wish you would catch the sonofabitch. My trade has dropped off considerably. About half of that garrison is scared to come into town late at night. Sure, I'll keep your secret. Keep that badge in your pocket as long as you want to."

He thought about telling her of his plans for the Castles, but then kept quiet. It wasn't necessary that she know everything just yet, but he did have some questions that he wanted to ask her about the family. He figured that she could give him more detailed information than anyone else, but right then he was concentrating on the best steak he had had in a long time and the several choices of desserts that would follow the meal.

There was no teasing, no coyness, no pretending reluctance that he might have encountered from a younger, less worldly woman. When the meal was finished and they had coffee and brandy, she simply took him by the hand and led him through a door into what obviously was her bedroom. It was very large, with one of the biggest beds that Longarm had ever seen, covered with a silk counterpane. The lighting was dim but adequate. She sat Longarm down on the bed and then standing right in front of him, slowly took her clothes off. She was wearing a frilly, lacy lavender gown that went well with her coloring. It was followed by several slips, until she was finally down to her camisole and the silk stockings that encased her legs.

It was done so unsexually that Longarm thought it was the most exciting, most sexual thing that he had ever seen. Her every movement was natural. She undressed as unconsciously and matter-of-factly as if she were in the room alone. He felt like she was giving him the chance to peek through her window late at night. Before she was half through, he found himself short of breath and his jeans uncomfortably tight. His neck was swelling and a coppery taste was coming into his mouth. As she finally slid the camisole over her breasts and then down over her long, sleek body, he thought that he was going to explode at the sight of her. Her skin was creamy and her breasts were large and plump, but yet she had a very slim belly with wide hips that tapered to straight rounded legs. The vee of her brush was starkly black against the soft mound that it grew on. She took a step toward him, and he leaned forward to kiss the smooth, soft, velvet skin of her belly. His lips moved up, seeking the nipples of her breasts. She bent slightly to accommodate him. His breathing was coming harder and harder. He slowly put his arms up and pulled her on the bed beside him. For a few moments they sat, he fully clothed, she naked. Their arms were around each other and they were kissing deeply and searchingly.

Almost as if they understood it to the second, he arose as she slowly began to push herself back up onto the bed. His undressing was not like hers. His was done in haste, as he ripped at the buttons of his shirt, yanked off his gunbelt, threw off his boots, and shrugged out of his jeans. In an instant, he was lying beside her on the soft silk of the counterpane that was almost as smooth and sleek as her skin. He started kissing her on the neck, letting his tongue run over her velvet skin. Slowly he worked his way down until his face was buried in the soft hair that grew on the soft little mound. He could smell and then taste the soft musk of her. She was beginning to groan. Her legs spread, growing wider and wider. Suddenly she reached up, took his head between her hands, and guided it as if it were an instrument to be used for her pleasure. In a moment, her hips were rising and falling rhythmically. Then she let out a low muffled shriek that suddenly rose louder and louder and louder, until it culminated in a sigh that descended and fell and descended some more.

For only a second was she relaxed. In an instant she had come up to him where he was kneeling on the side of the bed and taken him inside her mouth. With a pulsating motion of her head, she drew and extracted and drew and extracted from him until he felt as if he was being sucked into the vortex of a whirlpool.

Somehow, without knowing how exactly, they were intertwined and he was inside her and her legs were up around his shoulders wrapped around his neck. He brought her up, thrusting into her. Thrusting and thrusting harder and harder. She pulled him closer and closer to her. He felt her come up and come up until just at the pinnacle, he slowed. She dug her fingernails fiercely into his back. He brought her back up again, only this time he let her keep going until she exploded—writhing and contorting her body and trembling so that he could barely hold her. Her scream was loud and primordial. It went on and on and on. He didn't know if he was screaming with her but suddenly, all that he could remember was that he was feeling totally spent.

He toppled off of her and lay exhausted beside her on the bed. For a long ten minutes, neither of them spoke or made a sound other than their breathing. Finally, Longarm shuddered and tried to sit up. She reached out a gentle hand and pushed him back down.

"Not yet," she said softly.

A quarter of an hour passed and he was suddenly aware that she had slipped out of bed. A few moments later, she was back wearing some sort of loose wrap and carrying two glasses of brandy. She had a cigarette and a match for him. He sat up gratefully as she slid in the bed beside him. To his left was a nightstand table that held an ashtray. He lit the cigarette and took a deep inhale, blew out the smoke, and then set the cigarette carefully in the ashtray. After that, they lay side by side against the headboard of the bed and sipped brandy.

He said, "Wow!"

She reached up and kissed him gently. "I don't want it very often, Longarm, but when I do, I want the best and I knew you were going to be the best."

He half smiled. "You may not want it very often, but when you want it, you want a whole bunch of it."

"Are you complaining?"

"Noooo . . . ma'am." He reached out and got his cigarette and took a drag. "Right now, I'm not complaining about anything except that I wish that I was ten years younger so I could get this thing back up again."

She laughed. "You know the best way to ruin a good thing?"

"Yeah, have too much of it at one time."

"Exactly right."

After a time, they slowly got up out of bed. Mabelle dressed in a simple silk lounging robe while Longarm was obliged to put on his clothes. He didn't bother to strap on his gunbelt, just slung it over his shoulder when they walked back into the dining room parlor area. They sat apart from each other across the small table. Mabelle poured them another glass of brandy and they sat back in some contentment.

After they had grown mellow, Longarm lit another cigarette. He said, "Mabelle, I'm gonna save you the trouble of having to wait any longer than you have to to find out what I am going to do. I'm gonna tell you about it because I want your opinion. You're a sagacious woman, you know this town, you know these people, you know where all the skeletons are, you know who is sleeping with who, and you know who is having to pay for it here because he ain't getting it at home."

Mabelle said, "I won't deny that I'm in the ideal position to know what goes on."

Longarm nodded slowly. "All that I can hope is that you're the only one who recognized me."

She shrugged so that the robe fell off one of her shoulders and bared half of her left breast. "I wouldn't give that any thought," she said. "Actually, I only had my suspicions when I first saw you in here the other night. I sent off a couple of telegrams to confirm what I thought to be the truth. No, I don't think that you need have any doubts about that."

"Well, after tomorrow—I'm hoping tomorrow—I don't think that it will make any difference."

"What do you mean, after tomorrow?"

He said, "I'm putting on the badge and I'm going after the Castles. What do you think of that?"

Mabelle Russell said slowly and with consideration, "I think that you are on shaky ground. I think that you better have all your facts. I think you better have the right bait on your hook. You don't want to fool with the Castles, Longarm, unless you are real certain. They are rich and they have powerful friends. That's a bad combination to go up against."

"I know that, Mabelle, but I've got no better suspects for the murder of these soldiers than the Castles."

She said impatiently, "I thought that we discussed that. Vernon Castle or even James Castle isn't stupid enough to think that killing a few soldiers is going to get that garrison moved. I don't know why they want the army out of here, but they do. But that still doesn't mean they're willing to kill soldiers one by one to do it. It just doesn't make any sense."

He looked up at her steadily. "I know it doesn't make any sense. It's an insane thing to do. Right?"

She said, "Yes. You'd have to be simpleminded."

"Do you know any of the Castles that are simpleminded?"

A frown suddenly creased the smooth skin between her eyes. She said, "Virgil?"

"Who else?"

She looked off in to space for a moment. "That's funny, I never thought of Virgil. Now, come to think of it, I've got every reason to think of Virgil. That silly sonofabitch damned near killed one of my girls about two years ago."

He said, "What? Almost killed one of your girls?"

"Yeah. His brothers brought him up here, my God. He's almost twenty-six or twenty-seven years old and had never had a woman before, so a couple of years back, they got him all washed and cleaned up. I won't let anybody in with any of my girls that hasn't had a bath that very day or shaved. They've got to be decent. I mean, my girls have feelings too. But you don't want to hear about that. Anyway, they brought him up here. I wasn't none too happy about it. He's not the most appealing person in the world because you never know what he is going to do. He ain't all that bad-looking, tall and skinny, but there is a certain look in his eyes like nobody's there, if you know what I mean."

Longarm said, "Yeah."

"So anyway, I turned him over to one of my more experienced girls, a little girl from Kansas City named Kathy. They went on back to the room and it wasn't fifteen minutes when we started hearing screaming. Now, you'll hear screaming around this place—some of it's real and some of it's not—I don't have to tell you how it is around a place like this."

Longarm smiled. "Yeah, I know."

She said, "Only this screaming was different. This screaming would have curdled your blood. Well, me and a couple of men that I keep around here to handle some situations went dashing back there and knocked the door down. That crazy sonofabitch had Kathy backed up in a corner, both of them naked as hell. He had a pair of wire cutters in his hand. Turns out the simple sonofabitch wanted to cut her nipples off. He claimed that he was an Indian of some kind. He said that was some kind of a rite, something that an Indian man did to his wife if she had been unfaithful to him, and he said that Kathy had been unfaithful."

Longarm looked puzzled. "He said all that? Why . . . how did he possibly think that Kathy had been . . . didn't he know where he was?"

Mabelle said, "Listen, don't ever try to figure out whatever goes on in that man's mind, if there is a mind in there. But he was going to punish her because he had seen another man come out of there before he had gone in and that's what Indians do. He really and truly thinks that he is an Indian. I don't know where he got onto this nonsense, but he had a pair of wire cutters."

"Where did he get the wire cutters?"

"Damned if I know. I guess he brought them with him. All I know is that he was planning on nipping off Kathy's nipples. Some sort of ancient rite, he said."

Longarm shook his head wonderingly. "Do you know of any other incidents with Virgil?"

Mabelle thought for a moment. "There's been a lot of little things. Of course, the old man always buys his way out. I charged the old man two thousand dollars for that little stunt. Gave it to Kathy, of course. It liked to scared the hell out of that little girl. Oh! And then there was the time when he stole a man's horse and led him out of town, cut the horse's throat, and was skinning the horse out. He was about to eat it raw when some riders came along and stopped him."

Longarm shook his head slowly. "That's Comanche. That's what the Comanches did. When they were in a hurry, when they were on the run, they would stop and cut steaks off a live horse and eat them. He must have heard about it from somewhere. I guess his daddy bought his way out of that one?"

"Of course. The sheriff even went along with it, though it was horse-thieving. I mean, you steal a horse to ride or you steal a horse to eat, it's still horse-thieving, ain't it?"

Longarm laughed. "That's the first time I've ever come across someone stealing a horse to eat him."

She said, "I don't know of any other big incidents. They keep him pretty close to home but he gets out and wanders around. I'm sure that you know about last night when he was found wandering alone with his rifle naked. He wasn't exactly naked, he was wearing one of those things that the Indians wear. Do you know what I mean?"

"It's a breech cloth."

"Yes, one of those."

Longarm thought for a minute. "Well, he's the best I've got, Mabelle. What do you think?"

She said, "I wouldn't put it past him. He wouldn't even need a reason. Maybe he thinks he is a Comanche Indian killing soldiers."

"I hadn't thought about that before, but then I didn't know that he thought he was a Comanche Indian."

She laughed. "No one knows where he got the idea. Of course, in his younger days there was still plenty of Comanche Indians around here. Maybe somebody scared him about the Comanches gonna get him when he was young or something. No, that couldn't be right. The Castles haven't been around this area that long. They came from somewhere in the Midwest. Hell, Longarm. He's just simpleminded. God only knows how his mind works."

Longarm left her not too long after that. Before he did, he kissed Mabelle tenderly and thanked her for one of the best evenings he could remember. He said, "You're a hell of a woman, Mabelle. Too bad you don't want a man full time."

She said, "Oh, men are like whiskey. A little goes a long way. Don't think that I don't like my fair share of it, though. The problem with a husband is that he begins to tell you what he wants you to do and how to act and think and talk. I'm not much of one to have someone tell me anything. I like being the boss, Longarm, or haven't you noticed?"

He laughed. "Oh, yes. I noticed."

Before he got out the door she said, putting her hand on his arm, "Listen, honey. You be careful with those Castles. They are dangerous, everyone of them, and they have a lot of hired hands out there. Don't expect any help from the sheriff."

He said dryly, "I hadn't counted on it. In fact, I figured that he would be on the other side. Before I go out and see the Castles, I'm gonna make him aware of the facts and make it clear to him what will happen if he interferes."

Then he shrugged. "Of course, all of this is just talk if I don't get a bench warrant from a federal judge in Nebraska that gives me the right to go out and arrest the Castles and search their premises."

"Why would you want to search their premises?"

"You never know what you might find, Mabelle. I'm just trying to put a little heat on the old man to make him give Virgil up. I think they are all aware that he is the one that is killing these soldiers. I think they are protecting him. I've got to make the price so high that Vernon Castle is willing to surrender his own son to save the rest of them."

Mabelle shook her head. "Well, all I can do is wish you luck."

Longarm's face was grim. "Just hope that I get that telegram. I just want the chance."

He spent the morning and the early part of the afternoon hanging around his hotel and fretting, hoping, waiting impatiently for an answer to the telegram he had sent to Omaha. At about three o'clock, a messenger from the telegraph office finally brought him the envelope that he had been waiting for. He gave the boy a half a dollar, and went to his room and opened it anxiously.

It was exactly what he had hoped for. It was an official bench warrant from a federal judge in Omaha empowering him to arrest the Castle brothers, their progeny, and any or all of their employees who might in any way be linked to the importation and sale of cattle brought into the United States by means other than those proscribed by the laws governing the introduction of livestock to the United States from foreign soil. He was further empowered to seize all assets or items that might in any way be construed to have been a part of this illegal operation. It further instructed any and all law enforcement authorities, be they local, county, state, or federal, to assist Deputy United States Marshal Custis Long in the furtherance of his duty. Failure to do so would subject those law officers to such charges as the federal judiciary might care to bring. It was signed by Judge J.P. Bridgewater.

There was a second telegram in the envelope. It was from Longarm's friend, the deputy in Omaha. It said simply:

THIS OUGHT TO SATISFY YOU STOP NOW, HOW ABOUT GIVING ME BACK MY HORSE AND WIFE STOP

• • •

Longarm chortled with glee at his friend's joke, but mainly at the bench warrant from the judge. Even though it was sent in the form of a telegram, it was as official as if it had been written by the judge's own hand.

He folded the telegram and put it into his shirt pocket. He strapped on his gunbelt and made ready to go have a quick visit with Sheriff Smith before going out to the Castle ranch. His intention was to apprehend the Vernon Castle family and then go after James Castle. He didn't think that he would bother with James Castle's young sons and daughters.

First he went around to the stable and gave instructions to have his chestnut saddled and left in front of the sheriff's office.

He walked across the street to Sheriff Smith's office. On the boardwalk, he stopped for a moment to take his badge out of his shirt pocket and pin it to the fabric. Then he opened the door and stepped inside. The sheriff was alone at his desk. He looked up in annoyance as Longarm walked toward him.

Sheriff Smith said, "I thought I told you to get the hell out of here. I don't want to see you or hear you or smell you."

For an answer, Longarm tapped his chest, directing the sheriff's attention toward the badge.

The sheriff peered and then fumbled around on his desk until he found his glasses. He put them on, curling them behind his ears, and stared at Longarm's chest. He said, "What the hell? You're a deputy U.S. marshal. What the hell do you mean coming into my town and not telling me you're here!"

Longarm said evenly, "Listen, Sheriff Smith, this is not

a real good time to get on my cross side. So you listen to me carefully. I am going out to arrest Vernon Castle and any of his sons that are in their right mind. I am going to arrest them for bringing illegal Mexican cattle into this state and selling them into the northern markets."

Sheriff Smith said, blustering, "You'll do no damn such thing. This is my county and nobody comes in here and arrests its citizens without my say-so. You got that, Marshal?"

Longarm tapped his badge. "Smith, my badge is bigger than yours. Don't give me no trouble. I'm going out to arrest the Castles and I'm going to bring them in and house them in your jail, do you understand me?"

Smith stood up. "The hell you will."

Longarm leaned forward. "Sheriff, you defy me and you had better be prepared to spend some time in a federal penitentiary."

Smith said, "You go to hell, mister."

Longarm reached into his pocket for the telegram. He said, "That is *Marshal* to you, Sheriff. Marshal Custis Long."

The sheriff looked puzzled. "Longarm?"

"You got it right. Now, take a look at this." He unfolded the telegram and spread it on the desk in front of the sheriff.

In order to read it, the sheriff was forced to sit back down. It took him several minutes. He read it and then reread it and then finally reread it one last time. He took his glasses off and looked up at Longarm. He said, "You sneaky sonofabitch."

Longarm said, "You better watch your mouth, Sheriff Smith. I already don't much care for your attitude. It wouldn't take much more to get me down on you. Now,

I'm going to go out to the Castles and when I bring them in here, you better be ready." He put out a finger and tapped the telegram. "You better be ready to comply with what that federal bench warrant says or I'll put you in one of your own cells. Do you understand that?"

The sheriff looked at him steadily. "There is just you. I've got two deputies and myself and I can get a few more deputies if I need them."

"Yes, and there is a fort full of soldiers out there and I can requisition them as fast as I can requisition a horse or a blanket from them. Now if you fool with me, you'll have federal marshals coming out of your ears. Do you understand that, Smith?"

The sheriff tried to stare back at Longarm for a second. His jaw muscles worked, but finally he dropped his eyes. "I hope that you know what the hell you are doing," he said. "You don't fool around with a family like the Castles that easily. You're going to cost me my job, dammit."

"Surprisingly enough, Sheriff, I don't give a damn about your job. You've had it too soft for too long. You've been serving the wrong master. You're supposed to be serving the voters of this county, not Vernon Castle or his brother James."

He reached out and took the telegram, folded it, and put it back in his pocket. "I will expect you to be here in this jail ready to receive prisoners in about two or three hours."

The sheriff said maliciously, "That is if you get off that ranch alive, which ain't all that sure."

Longarm turned for the door. "Well, I reckon that you had better let me worry about that."

Chapter 8

Longarm approached the Vernon Castle ranch headquarters warily. There was a big gate and a fence that led to the ranch house. He stopped in the opening and studied the lay of the land. He could see a few cattle and a few cowhands working off in the distance. His objective was to catch all four of the immediate family together at the same time. It was just after five o'clock. His hope was that they would be in from the day's work and would be having a drink before dinner.

He started up the road that led to the whitewashed house with the red tile roof. As he neared, he could see that it had a big wide front porch. He saw no one hanging about near the place.

When he reached the front of the house, he dropped his reins and dismounted slowly. He thought of taking his rifle into the house, but decided against it. He wanted to get in and look around before he let them know that his intentions were hostile.

There was a big brass knocker on the wooden front door. He rapped it loudly. After a few moments, it was answered by a Mexican lady, a servant most likely.

Longarm said, "Señor Vernon Castle, please."

She nodded as if she didn't speak much English and pulled the door open and stepped aside. Longarm walked into the big, cool interior of the front room. It was styled with a high ceiling and filled with heavy Mexican furniture.

Longarm said, "Is Señor Castle here?"

The woman nodded, backing away. She said, "Sí, sí. Señor Castle is *aqui. Yo venga.*"

Longarm figured she wanted him to follow her. They were just crossing the big parlor when a man stepped out from a side room. He was tall and well built, with a shock of white hair. He was well dressed and looked as if he belonged.

Longarm said, "Mr. Castle?"

The man looked at him inquiringly. "Yes, and who might you be?"

Longarm said, "I'm Deputy United States Marshal Custis Long. I'm here to arrest you and your sons for the theft and illegal importation of Mexican cattle. I have a bench warrant from a judge in Omaha, Nebraska."

Vernon Castle reacted as if he had been slapped in the face with a two-by-four. He went ashen white and staggered backwards a foot. He said, "What? You've got what?"

Longarm said, "Where are your sons?"

Vernon Castle said, "You haven't got any damn warrant for my arrest. I haven't been in Omaha in two years."

"You don't have to be in Omaha, just the cattle that you brought into this country illegally. Whether you stole them or not is another matter, but you brought them into this country illegally and you shipped them to Omaha as American-bred cattle. That is a felony and you are now under arrest for it. I ask you again, where are your sons? They are also fugitives. If you harbor fugitives, that is a second felony."

Castle was trying hard to regain his composure. He looked around wildly and said, "I don't know where they are."

Longarm said, "Then let's go into your office and wait for them."

Castle thought for a moment and then backed toward the door he had just exited from. He said, "All right, but—"

Before he could finish the sentence, a door slammed in the back part of the house and there was the sound of heavy boots and the jingling of spurs. Both Vernon Castle and Longarm froze.

Vernon Castle started to open his mouth. Longarm put a finger to his lips. Before Vernon Castle could speak, Billy Bob Castle and his brother Glenn came walking into the big parlor. They stopped instantly when they saw Longarm. They were perhaps ten yards away. For a second they stared at him, and then recognition dawned on both, almost at the same time. A gleam came into the heavy face of Billy Bob. He started forward. Vernon Castle was not armed, but both of his sons were wearing gunbelts.

Longarm put out a hand. "Stop right there!" he said. "My name is Custis Long and I am a deputy U.S. marshal and you are both under the arrest for the theft and illegal importation of Mexican cattle. Remove those gunbelts and drop them on the floor."

120

They stared at him in disbelief, their eyes finally settling on the badge on his chest. They looked at one another and then back at Longarm. Glenn Castle said to his father, "Dad, is he telling the truth? What is this all about?"

Longarm reached into his pocket and pulled out the telegram. He said, "I have here a bench warrant from a judge in Omaha, Nebraska, calling for your arrest and extradition to that state to face charges for the illegal importation of cattle to the United States. I told you to drop those gunbelts."

For a second or two nothing happened, and then Glenn and Billy Bob slowly began to draw away from each other, forming with their father a half circle around Longarm. It was clear to the deputy what they were doing. He drew his revolver, pulling back the hammer as he did.

He said, "Stop! Hold it! Hold it!"

Vernon Castle said, "Do what he says boys. He looks just crazy enough to shoot." He glared at Longarm. "Do you have any idea how many judges and senators and state representatives and United States representatives I know? Mister, your ass is going to be in a sling made out of barbed wire before I am through with you."

Longarm said, "That may be so, but right now I am running things. Now, bunch together. I'm not going to tell you again to get those gunbelts off."

The two young men looked questioningly at their father. He said, "Do what he wants for the time being, boys. We'll let the lawyers work this out. Let's just don't have anybody get hurt accidentally by this gun-happy fool."

Watching Longarm, they carefully unbuckled their gunbelts and carefully lowered them to the floor. Then they straightened back up and glared at Longarm.

Billy Bob said, "Well, now, Mr. Gunwhipper. What now?"

Longarm took several steps toward them. "Now we go into the office and talk. Maybe something can be worked out here."

He sensed something behind him and knew that he was going to be attacked before he heard the sound. He guessed that it was something he saw in the three men's eyes. All of a sudden, a body came driving into him from behind. The weight of the impact threw him to the left and toward the floor. As he was falling, he saw Glenn leaning down for his revolver. With his arm partly restricted by whoever was wrestling him to the ground, Longarm fired just before he hit the floor. He saw the bullet hit Glenn in the thigh, knocking his legs out from under him.

The force of their two bodies striking the tile floor caused Longarm's assailant to lose his grip. In a second, Longarm had elbowed and kicked backward until he was free. He jumped to his feet quickly, covering Vernon Castle and his two sons. He took two steps backwards so that he could see his assailant and still keep an eye on the others.

On the floor was a man he took to be Virgil Castle. He was tall and thinly muscular, wearing a pair of blue jeans. Other than that, he was unclothed. He was barefoot, he wore no shirt, and his hair was long and stringy.

Longarm asked Vernon Castle, "Who the hell is that?"

Vernon Castle said, "That's my son Virgil."

Longarm said, "Tell him to get the hell out of here or I'll arrest him for obstruction of justice and assaulting a federal officer in the performance of his duty."

The man got to his feet, staring at Longarm. Now Longarm could see what Mabelle had meant by the look in the simpleton's eyes. They did indeed look like there was no one there. They were vacant and staring.

Vernon Castle said, "Son. Go on outside. Go on outside right now."

Virgil Castle said, "What's going on, Daddy?" His voice was deep. He sounded like a man and he looked like a man, but the way he said his words it was as if he were a small child. "Is this man trying to hurt ya'll?" He indicated Longarm. "I won't let him hurt ya'll if ya'll don't want him to."

Vernon Castle said urgently, "Son, your brother is hurt. Get outside and get someone to come in and help. Hurry."

Longarm watched the tall, lanky man with the dirty, stringy hair disappear out the front door. Then he watched while Vernon and Billy Bob went to where Glenn was down on the floor. A small pool of blood was outlined against the gray tile of the living room floor.

Longarm could see that the slug had gone in just to the side of Glenn Castle's left leg. It looked to be no more than a flesh wound. The bullet had gone right through.

Longarm said, "Get a handkerchief and put a tourniquet up around near his hip. Hell, he ain't hurt. I've seen steaks hurt worse than that sent back to the kitchen to get cooked some more."

Vernon Castle turned a furious face toward Longarm. He was red with rage. "By God, sir. You have shot my son, you sonofabitch. You will damn well pay for this. You may damn well not get off this ranch alive."

Longarm slowly pulled the hammer of his revolver back to the firing position. It went *clitch-clatch*. He said, "Mr. Castle, you are under arrest. Your sons are under arrest. Your son went for a weapon while being arrested by a federal marshal. You'd better be thankful for one thing, Mr. Castle, that I didn't get a clean shot at him. I meant to shoot him straight through the chest. Do you understand me? If I hadn't been falling, I wouldn't have missed. As far as I'm concerned, I missed. You got that?"

Castle stood there, his face contorted. He said coldly, "I'll get you for this, you sonofabitch."

"You better see to your son's leg. We've got a long ride into town and this little nick he's got ain't gonna interfere with it."

The huge man called Billy Bob was kneeling by his brother's leg. By this time, Glenn Castle was sitting up. He was staring at Longarm fixedly. Hate filled his eyes.

Billy Bob said, "I'm going to squash you till you ain't no higher than a pancake, mister."

Longarm smiled. "Last time you tried that, you almost got some brains beat into your head. I had hoped that it would take."

At that instant, Virgil Castle returned with two cowhands. They came in and stopped, looking startled at what they saw.

One of the cowhands said, "Mr. Castle, what in the hell is going on?"

They both glanced at Longarm holding the pistol on the father and the two sons. One of them moved his hand an inch or two toward his own revolver.

Longarm said, "Don't do anything sudden or foolish, son. I am a deputy United States marshal. I am arresting these men. You are directed right now to get outside and hitch up a buckboard. I am taking them to town with me. Spread the word among the other people that work here on this ranch. If there is any interference with the United States marshal in the performance of his duty, the first man that gets shot is going to be Mr. Vernon Castle. Is that clear?"

They stared at him, open-mouthed. Then one of them turned back to Vernon Castle and said, "Boss, what are we supposed to do?"

Vernon Castle said through clenched teeth, "For the time being, do what he tells you. We'll get this all straightened out with the sheriff in town." He turned to look at Longarm. "And then we'll get this hash settled once and for all."

Longarm said, "Now for the last time, you two men get out of here and get a buggy hitched. Bring it around to the front. I've got a wounded man in here. You savvy?"

Vernon Castle said, "Yes, Tom. Hurry up and get that buggy around. We need to get Glenn into a doctor. Make it a buckboard so he can stretch out."

The two cowhands nodded and then departed. Virgil Castle just stood there. Longarm said, "You." He motioned at Virgil. "Get over there with the rest of your family."

Virgil stared at him as if he didn't understand what he meant. Vernon Castle erupted into anger. He said, "Oh, no. No, no. You can well see that my son couldn't be guilty of anything. He is a child, Marshal. Surely you're not taking him in."

Longarm appeared to be adamant. He said, "Why shouldn't I? He's one of the bunch. Doesn't he help run the family business?"

Vernon Castle said desperately, "My God, man. Look at him. Listen to him. Does he sound like he helps run the business? He's a child."

"Well, what am I supposed to do with him? Just leave him here?"

"For God's sake, man. Just leave him alone. Leave him here. The people on the ranch will look after him. They understand him."

Longarm asked, "You gonna guarantee no trouble if I leave him here?"

"Yes, yes, yes. Yes, we'll go along quietly. We'll get this matter settled in town, but for heaven's sakes, leave the boy alone."

Longarm said with a grudging sound in his voice, "Well, all right, but if he is in any way involved in this cattle business, you'll be the loser in it."

Vernon Castle said, "Oh, damn, man. Would you stop this business about illegal cattle. Nobody's involved in anything."

"You heard the charges and you can bet that I intend to get to the bottom of it." As he said it, he knew they were thinking only about the business of illegally imported cattle. They would have no way of knowing the whole operation was aimed at catching the murderers of the U.S. Cavalry soldiers.

Longarm said, "All right, I hear that buckboard coming. Ya'll get that boy on his feet and ya'll start toward the front door." He motioned with his gun. "And if anybody gets cute, it will be the last time they get a chance to do anything. Do you understand me?"

For answer, they stared at him with hate in their eyes. He decided right then and there that the Castles were just a little bit spoiled.

With the grudging, almost rebellious cooperation of the sheriff, Longarm finally got his prisoners housed in the jail. He put the two brothers in one cell and their father in another directly across from them. A doctor had been called in to see to Glenn's wound. As Longarm had guessed, it was very slight—just a furrow along the outside of his thigh. Not much deeper than you could have laid a finger in. The doctor didn't speak much except about the wound, but he seemed extremely puzzled as to what such a powerful family was doing in jail. Longarm made it clear that he should finish his business as fast as possible and get out and that he was under federal orders to keep his mouth shut.

Almost as soon as the door had shut on his cell, Vernon Castle had begun clamoring for his lawyer. He now told the sheriff, "Get Botts. Get Clarence Botts over here immediately. We don't want to stay in these cells any longer than we have to. Do you understand me, Sheriff? Get over there and get me Clarence Botts."

Longarm said, "I don't know if it's in the rules that you can send a law officer to fetch your lawyer. I'm not at all certain about that." But he was just saying it for effect. He knew the problem that the lawyer was going to run into better than Mr. Castle did. Mr. Castle didn't know it, but he was going to be in the jail cell a lot longer than he could ever expect.

Sheriff Smith said belligerently to Longarm, "Listen, Marshal, you sonofabitch. You can't order me around. If I want to go get this man his lawyer, then I'm going to go get this man his lawyer."

Longarm fixed the sheriff with an icy look. "I have a feeling, Sheriff Smith, that you are going to be occupying one of these cells yourself before this is all over with."

"You go to hell."

The sheriff turned on his heel, marched down the line of cells, and went out into his outer office, slamming the lockup door behind him.

Longarm had shown the telegram warrant to Vernon Castle and his two sons. Mr. Castle had immediately questioned the legality of a warrant sent by telegram. Longarm had assured him that it was legal and that his lawyer would so advise him as soon as he arrived.

The lawyer was not long in coming. Perhaps ten minutes passed after the sheriff left before a short, balding man came bustling down the line of cells saying, "All right, what is this all about? I demand to know what this is all about right now."

Longarm said, "My name is Custis Long. I am a deputy U.S. marshal out of Denver, Colorado. You must be the lawyer of these accused parties."

The little man was almost stuttering he was so upset. "I am. I am Clarence Botts. What right do you have to place these prominent citizens of this town in this jail?"

Longarm answered, "By the power of the United States federal government."

Botts said, "I don't care if you're a deputy sheriff to the President of the United States. You have no right arresting a man like Vernon Castle."

From his cell, Vernon Castle said, "Clarence, get us out of here. The man has some sort of bogus telegram from a federal judge. Just get us the hell out of here."

Mr. Botts said placatingly, "Mr. Castle, I will have you out of here within the hour. You can be assured of that."

Longarm reached for his pocket and took out the warrant. He said, "I wouldn't be quite so sure about all that, Mr. Botts. You better read this. It's from a federal judge out of Omaha, Nebraska."

While Botts was reading the telegram and reading it again and rereading it, Longarm stood serenely by. He figured that he was much more experienced in such matters than the small-town lawyer. What the lawyer was about to find out was that no local judge could vacate the warrant or set bail. That could only be done by a federal judge, and the nearest federal judge was 150 miles away.

Mr. Botts finished reading the telegram and cleared his throat several times. He looked at Mr. Castle and said, "Mr. Castle, I want you to be very understanding about something, sir."

Chapter 9

Vernon Castle was so angry that he could hardly speak. He said, "What do you mean you've got to get to a federal judge to get us out of this damn jail. Get over to Judge Watkins. Get him to set bail or to release me immediately. My God, when I think of the money I've contributed to that man's campaign."

Mr. Botts was clearly uncomfortable giving Mr. Castle bad news. He said, "You see, that's just it. Judge Watkins is a state judge, a circuit judge. I've got to get to a federal judge in San Antonio."

Vernon Castle was staggered. He shouted, "San Antonio! My God, that will take you twenty-four hours!"

Longarm said mildly, "It's gonna take you a little longer than that. Federal judges don't just vacate other judges' warrants without good cause. There'll have to be some correspondence between that judge and the one in Omaha. I think that you'd better just settle down for a nice stay."

Vernon Castle stared at his lawyer. "Clarence, does this man know what he is talking about?"

Botts ducked his head. "I am afraid so, Mr. Castle."

Across the way, Billy Bob was up, gripping the bars of his cell with his huge hands. He shook the door so that it clanked and rattled. He said, "Goddamnit, Paw. We got to get out of here. I can't stand being locked up like this. I can't stand it. You've gotta get us out of here."

Vernon Castle looked at him. "Billy Bob," he said, "I don't need none of that right now. You settle down. You hush, you hear? Settle down like Glenn is. Let me work on this." He turned his attention back to his lawyer. He said with menace in his voice, "Botts, you contact every important man I know and you cascade that judge in San Antonio with telegrams from those people. You be on the next train outta here for San Antonio. Do you see me? Do you see the fact that I am standing in a jail cell where God knows what vermin have been? And this man"—he jabbed his finger maliciously at Longarm—"is responsible. I want it stated right here and now that I will have this sonofabitch's badge, if not his head."

Longarm said calmly, "Better walk easy there, Mr. Castle. You are coming mighty close to threatening a law officer."

Vernon Castle said, "You go to hell." He switched back to the lawyer. "Clarence, get moving! Now! Do whatever you have to do, just get us out of here!"

Clarence Botts turned to Longarm. He said, "I need that warrant."

Longarm laughed. "Not very damn likely," he said. "I'll let you write out a copy of it if you want, but I'm not about to give you this official copy. This is the same as if it were taken from the hand of the judge himself."

Botts said, "All right, let's go into the sheriff's office so I can make a copy."

Longarm and the lawyer walked out to where the sheriff was sitting morosely at his desk. When he understood what the lawyer wanted, he provided writing materials and watched as Mr. Botts wrote out the telegram meticulously, word for word. When he was through, Mr. Botts folded the copy and put it in his pocket.

Botts said to the sheriff, "Please, please. Try to settle Mr. Castle down. Make him just as comfortable as you possibly can. I'll be back just as soon as I can."

Sheriff Smith glared at Longarm. "There ain't much I can do," he said. "This is the sonofabitch that is making him uncomfortable."

Longarm said, "I believe that's about the thirtieth time that I have been called a sonofabitch in the last hour. When it gets to fifty, I may go to doing something about it."

Mr. Botts said to Longarm, "Marshal, you may have bitten off a little more than you can chew."

"Oh, I don't know about that, Mr. Botts. A lot of people have told me that I have a big mouth."

Longarm watched as the frantic, plump little lawyer hurried out the door. Then he turned his eyes on the sheriff. "Sheriff Smith," he said, "I am going leave right now and I want to make one thing real clear to you. When I come back—and I could come back anytime night or day—those Castle people had better be where I left them just now. If they ain't, you're gonna replace them. Do you understand me?"

Sheriff Smith looked at Longarm with venom in his eyes. He said, "For right now, and just for right now, you are holding the best cards. But there will be a new deal soon enough."

"Maybe so, and maybe not. This may be the last hand for all you know."

The sheriff said, "You forget one thing, Marshal. You ain't but one man. This town is solid behind the Castles."

"And you forget just one thing, Sheriff. I ain't just one man—there's a hundred and twenty troopers out there at the fort. I can requisition every damn one of them and put this town under martial law if I want to. That would include you." He leaned toward the sheriff. "Do you understand me?"

The sheriff turned away and walked to the other side of his office, staring out. He said, "I can't tell you to get out of here, but I wish the hell you would."

Longarm said, "Well, for once we are in agreement." He turned on his heel and went out the front door.

Even though it was coming dark, he rode straight to the fort and went in to see the captain, this time wearing his badge. In a very brief time he told the captain what had transpired.

Captain Montrose said, "And you think it's this Virgil Castle?"

"He's the best suspect I got. For a while, I thought it was an old man that lives about a mile from here named Clell Martin. Do you know him?"

The captain said, "Yes, he hates soldiers. I think he's an old Johnny Reb. I never considered he'd do something like this. He's all stove up from what I've heard. But I don't understand why you think that Virgil Castle would do this. Because he's simpleminded?"

"You're not going to believe this, but I think he thinks he is an Indian. I really believe that he is still fighting the horse soldiers."

Captain Montrose looked at him incredulously. "You

mean, you think a demented half-wit has been shooting my men because he is still fighting the Indian wars?"

"Well, this is an Indian fort, isn't it?"

"Don't talk rubbish, Marshal. We don't have any Indians around here. My God." He stood up and said, "Well, what do you want us to do? Do you want me to restrict my troopers to the garrison?"

Longarm said, "Captain, I've been thinking about that, giving it considerable thought, and I am of two minds. One, if you don't have any troopers out, I can't catch him in the act. But if you do, he is liable to kill somebody else. I'm going to try to watch him—that's the reason I left him out of jail, so I could watch him. But I don't know if I can keep that close an eye on him. He runs along on foot as far as I can tell. This is rough country. I'm not as young as I used to be. If I try to follow him on a horse, he is gonna see me. What do you think? Do you want to risk your troopers?"

Captain Montrose thought about it for a few moments. He said, "Why don't I restrict them for a couple of days and see what happens."

Longarm said, "Well, I ain't going to be able to tell much if you do that. I need to see if he will go for a position where he could shoot a trooper coming from town or going."

The captain said, "I don't understand why you didn't arrest the other Castle family."

Longarm said, "I had no real reason. I have no real suspicion of them. I have created enough trouble for myself arresting Vernon Castle and his two sons just to cut him off and isolate him. I really couldn't work up a healthy appetite for arresting James Castle. His children are young. My plan now, though, is that I'm going to go to work on Vernon and try to make him give Virgil up. I don't know if he suspects Virgil of doing this, or if he knows he's doing this or what, but he's not liking that jail at all. So I am going to be pounding on him and trying to convince him that the boy will be better off— I say boy, but really he is a man—that Virgil would be better off in one of those asylums than running around the country shooting people because sooner or later, someone is gonna wind up shooting *him*."

Captain Montrose said, "I will be guided by whatever you say, Marshal. I tell you, this is a very frustrating situation."

"I couldn't agree with you more. The one thing that I do want you to do, Captain Montrose, is that if there is any trouble, any trouble at all, of any kind, I do not want you to deal with it yourself. You will be dealing with civilians and that is my job. I want you to get word to me as fast as you can. I'll either be somewhere in town or I'll be hid out somewhere along the road that circles to the south, to James Castle's ranch, and the one up north of here, to Vernon Castle's ranch. I will be most likely somewhere near Vernon Castle's ranch or around town somewhere. If I am around town, I will most likely be at the jail or somewhere around my hotel."

Captain Montrose said, "All right. My God. I hope this will be the end of this."

That night, Longarm rode out to Vernon Castle's ranch, to a position about a quarter of a mile from the main gate. He stayed for several hours, watching. He felt that it was nothing more than a futile gesture, however. Virgil could slip away from the ranch at any point as much as a mile from the gate and he, Longarm, would never be aware. In his own mind, he thought his best chance was to hammer down on the old man and make him give his son up. It was the most hopeful outcome of the plan that he had put in motion.

He hadn't brought it up to Vernon Castle before because he wanted the old man and his two sons to have plenty of time to stew in their own juices. He figured that every minute they spent in that jail was a minute that would bring them closer to being cooperative. He was convinced the killer had to be Virgil Castle. If he was wrong, he had gone to a great deal of trouble and alienated a powerful man for nothing. Naturally, he had no intention of pursuing the charges of illegal cattle importation. All he was using that for was as a lever, as an ax, as a wedge, to try to force the old man into doing something alien to his nature.

He went over to the jail the next day, and let himself into the cells through the lockup door paying no attention to the sheriff. He walked back and stood in front of Vernon Castle's cell. The man was seated on his bunk. He looked distinctly uncomfortable and very angry. A day's worth of whisker growth was on his cheeks.

He glared up at Longarm. "Well, have you come to your senses and decided to let us out of here? I want you to know that my son is in considerable pain."

Longarm said, "Well, that's better than those five soldiers that got killed. They ain't in no pain at all. They ain't in nothing except a wooden box."

Vernon Castle gave him a look. He said, "What the hell are you talking about?"

"I'm talking about the soldiers that have been shot. Haven't you been moving heaven and earth to get that garrison out of here?"

Castle's face clouded. "What the hell does that have to do with me?"

"Who the hell would want the soldiers out of here more than the man who is killing them? That's one way of getting them out of here, isn't it?"

Vernon Castle's mouth dropped. "Are you crazy? Are you insane? Are you suggesting that I have been shooting U.S. Cavalry soldiers?"

Longarm asked, "Haven't you had the mayor and the city council and all of the citizens around here kicking up a ruckus to get that fort closed?"

Vernon stood up and came to the cell door. He said stiffly, "One has nothing to do with the other. I am trying to get that garrison out of here for reasons you wouldn't understand, and I have no intention of telling you. But I'm not fool enough to kill soldiers in order to move them."

Longarm turned his head and looked into the opposite cell to where Glenn and Billy Bob were sitting. He said, "Maybe you ain't fool enough, but you may have a son that is."

Billy Bob said, "Why, you crazy sonofabitch."

Vernon Castle said, "Shut up, son. I will tend to this man." He looked at Longarm. "Is that what this is all about? You think that I have been having those soldiers killed or that I have been killing them? That is why you've put me in jail? This isn't about illegal cattle, is it? It's not, is it?"

Longarm grinned for a moment. "No, but it's a charge that I can make stick. And all three of you can get fifteen years for it. I haven't brought your brother, James, into this yet. But the whole pack of you could get fifteen years because you all shipped cattle in common. So when I bring him in, that will be four of you going up for fifteen years."

Vernon Castle said, "You can't mean that!"

Longarm grinned. "Oh, yes, I can, and I do. Unless you agree to one thing."

Vernon Castle's face got guarded. "Agree to what?"

"Agree to give up the son who is doing the killing. You know it and I know it."

"What are you talking about?"

"I'm talking about Virgil."

For the second time, Vernon Castle's mouth dropped open. He sputtered for a moment and then said, "Virgil? Virgil? Do you think that Virgil is capable of killing soldiers? My God, man, he keeps *rabbits*! Go out to my ranch, man, and look behind the barn. He's got a pen of rabbits. He's as gentle as a child."

"He also runs around at night wearing a breechcloth and carrying a rifle."

"He is playing. He doesn't have any bullets in that rifle."

"So you say."

Vernon Castle looked frustrated. "Mr. Long, I don't know what I can say to convince you that you are way off the track. The very idea that you are holding me and my two sons here because you think that my other son is a murderer. You, sir, are the madman. You are the lunatic."

"Virgil thinks he is an Indian, doesn't he?"

Vernon Castle said, "I'm not even gonna dignify that with a reply. That is just absurd."

Longarm turned sideways so that he could see into the cell where Billy Bob and Glenn were listening. He said, "Oh, is that right? What about the night two years ago when his two brothers took him up to Mabelle Russell's whorehouse and he had a pair of wire cutters with him and he was going to nip off the two nipples of a young lady there—a lady by the name of Kathy, I believe it was."

Vernon Castle said, "That was greatly exaggerated."

Longarm looked at Billy Bob and Glenn and said, "Was it, boys? You were there. Wasn't he trying to cut off her nipples with those wire cutters?"

They both looked down and didn't say anything. Longarm turned to face Vernon Castle and said, "It's part of the Comanche creed that they disfigure any of their wives who are caught with another brave. Virgil saw a man coming out of that room where he was going in to get his cherry popped—with, as far as he was concerned, his bride."

Vernon Castle said, "This is preposterous."

Longarm looked at Glenn. "Didn't you boys tell him that he was going to get married that night?"

They still would not look up.

Longarm said to Vernon Castle, "And what about the fact that he tried to cut a steak off a horse after cutting its throat? That's an old Comanche trick also. When they are hard-pressed and there is enemy right behind them and they don't have time to stop and eat properly, they just cut a steak off a horse's haunch and keep riding on. What about that?"

Vernon Castle began to tremble. He went and sat back down. His voice was not as strong when he said, "I tell you, you are on the wrong track. The boy is touched but he is as harmless as a kitten. He wouldn't do such a thing. I would know if he did. Holding us here is not benefiting anyone. If he is a danger, the worst thing that you can do is to hold us in this cell where we can't take care of him."

"Well," Longarm said, "you think on it. Meanwhile, you are still facing fifteen years on this cattle business. I wouldn't be looking for Mr. Botts to be back in here with any good news any time soon. You're in a little deeper web than you think you are."

He turned and started out of the jail. Vernon Castle called out after him. "Marshal, surely there is something that can be worked out here. Surely there is something you want, something that we can trade for. You don't believe that we are guilty of illegal cattle transportation for a second."

Longarm laughed. "Oh, hell. Don't kid me. I know damn good and well that you have been mixing Mexican cattle in with yours and shipping them north, but that's common practice and nobody ever enforces the law. I'm not arresting you for that. I am arresting you to make you give up that son of yours—that murderous son of yours. I am arresting you because you are the father of a murderer."

Vernon Castle's voice was intense as he said, "There must be something that you want."

Longarm smiled. "Like money?"

Vernon Castle licked his lips. "Something might could be arranged." His eyes darted back and forth.

Longarm said, "Well, there is one thing that I want."

"What is it?"

"I want the murderer of those five soldiers. I don't count the one in the alley, but I want the murderer who has been shooting them out of the saddle, and I think it's Virgil. Give him up and I'll turn you loose. He'll be taken care of."

Vernon Castle's face twisted with anger. He said, "You go to hell, you sonofabitch. I'll see you out of this town, out of this state, and out of any possible job in government service before I am through with you."

Longarm gave him a wave as he walked out into the

outer office through the lockup door. As he passed through the outer office, he didn't bother to nod at the sheriff. Their declared hostilities were still in force.

For two nights, Longarm watched and patrolled and hid out wherever he thought that Virgil Castle might be lurking, but his efforts were futile. Captain Montrose had not imposed a restriction on his soldiers going into town, but they were no longer seen on the road. They were fearful, and Longarm couldn't blame them. But he did need them moving about. However, he could hardly go to them and ask if a few would ride back from town late at night so he could flush out a murderer. He didn't reckon that they would take too kindly to being used as bait.

On the morning of the fourth day, he went in to see Mr. Castle again, hoping that the man could be further persuaded to give Virgil up in some manner. There had been no further killings. Of course, that proved nothing.

Mr. Castle was obviously miserable from his stay in the jail. His sons were frantic and nervous. Longarm could tell from smelling their breaths that the sheriff had been sneaking whiskey in to them. He supposed that there were some things that even a deputy U.S. marshal shouldn't try to put a stop to.

He brought a chair with him on this visit, and he sat down facing Mr. Castle. "Mr. Castle," he said, "your lawyer's not back, and he's not going to be back for quite a while. Even when he gets back, he's not going to be able to get you out of this jail. You're in for a long stay unless you agree to cooperate."

Vernon Castle held his head in his hands and looked miserable. He said, "How can I convince you that Virgil is not capable of doing something like this? He's not capable of murder. He couldn't do something like this."

"Oh, he could cut a whore's tits off, but he couldn't murder a soldier. Is that what you are saying? Hell, Vernon. He thinks that he is a damn Comanche Injun. He's running around in a breechcloth. My God, he's not a child."

Castle said, "Did you see the rabbits? Did you go behind the barn and look at the rabbits he keeps? He's a gentle soul, he likes little things, little bunny rabbits, for heaven's sake."

"No, I didn't go see the bunny rabbits. But I did go into your office and I saw your gun rack. You've got four Hawken buffalo rifles, you've got four Sharps buffalo rifles, and you've got about six Springfields. You've got a whole stock of long-range, high-caliber rifles and that's what every one of those soldiers were killed with. Now I know that you say Virgil runs around with a carbine in his hand that hasn't got any cartridges in it. That's fine and dandy, but what's to keep him from taking down one of those Hawkens, one of those Sharps, or one of those Springfields and using it some dark night? Some of them soldiers were killed long after you went to bed. Just how close of a tab do you keep on Virgil, Mr. Castle?"

Vernon Castle raised a tired and haggard face. He said, "Nothing is going to convince you, is it, Marshal Long. You are convinced my boy is a murderer because he is simpleminded. You're convinced my family has a part in the killing of those soldiers because we have tried to get that fort moved. Isn't that the case?"

"That's a good place to start. I can't think of anyone else who has as much interest in that fort as you have."

"What if I told you the real reason that I was trying to get that fort moved? Would that make any difference to you?"

"That depends on the reason."

"If I tell you, you cost me the advantage of being the

only one who knows how valuable that land really is. But if it will get you to stop persecuting my family, and especially my son, then I will tell you. Will it? If I tell you and it makes sense to you, will you release us and will you leave my son Virgil alone?"

Longarm thought for a moment. He got up. "What if it doesn't convince me, Mr. Castle? What if your reasoning doesn't make any sense to me? What if I am still convinced that Virgil is the man who killed those soldiers? What then?"

Vernon Castle stood up and came to the bars. "It's got to convince you," he said. "It will make sense. You will see my reasoning. You will see that I would have no reason to call attention to that fort by murdering soldiers. That is the last thing I would want to happen. I'm not fool enough to think that I can run the army off that garrison if soldiers are being killed there."

"I never thought that you were that kind of a fool, Mr. Castle, but you see, I think that your son overheard you wanting that garrison moved and I think that he is fool enough to think that by killing them one at a time they would move that fort. I think that you inadvertently caused him to kill those soldiers. Now you can tell me the reason why you want that garrison moved—it doesn't make any difference to me. What does make a difference to me is that I think that your son Virgil is trying to please you by killing those soldiers."

Vernon Castle shook his violently. "He knows nothing about it. He hasn't heard a word from me about this. We don't take him into the family councils. We treat him for what he is—he's like a six-year-old child. Marshal. You've got to understand, he's not part of the family in that way, in the business way."

Longarm thought for a long moment. "O.K., fine. What is your reason for wanting that garrison moved?"

Vernon Castle stared into Longarm's eyes for a long time. Then he said, "Never mind. Not now. You're not ready to hear it. It wouldn't make any difference to you. I'll wait for my lawyer to get back. There is a great deal of money involved here. You're gonna do what you're gonna do anyway."

Longarm got up. He said to the man behind the bars, "You do whatever you think is best for you and yours. I am going to do my job. I wish you good luck, but I wouldn't be looking for this matter to be settled anytime soon." He started for the door. Halfway there, he stopped and looked back. "You mentioned that there was a great deal of money involved. That seems to be your greatest interest here. Your son is out there doing God knows what. There are soldiers being murdered out there—I think your son is the one doing it—and you're talking to me about money. You're some kind of a father, Mr. Castle, and an upstanding citizen on top of it. Good day to you, sir."

As he left through the lockup door he could hear shouted curses being hurled at him by all three of the Castles. He slammed the door behind him. The sheriff looked up as he passed. Longarm said without looking at him, "And the same to you too, Sheriff." He passed on out the front door and mounted his horse.

He rode south out of town making the big circle that he had ridden so many times the past few days. As he rode, he realized that the job was getting tougher and tougher. His sleep was being seriously interfered with by the nighttime vigils he was keeping. He had to snatch meals, his drinking time had seriously been cut into, and there had been no time for continued congeniality with

Miss Mabelle Russell. All in all, he thought it was one of the worst jobs that he had ever had. He hoped Billy Vail was happy.

But the job had produced a streak of stubbornness in him. It appeared to him to come down to a privileged family that thought they were going to take matters into their own hands. His job was to see that that sort of thing didn't happen, and he took it as sort of a personal affront to deal with people like Vernon Castle and be called a sonofabitch with such regularity.

He rode on past the James Castle ranch thinking that next day he just might go out and arrest *him*. He continued on around on the east side of the big loop fronting around San Angelo. As he came up toward the north, he could see a small figure by the side of the road. He put the chestnut into a lope, and the figure grew larger as he kicked up dust along the road.

Two hundred yards off, he could tell that it was Virgil Castle. One hundred yards away, he could see that he was squatting by the side of the road and was wearing nothing but a pair of Levi's. Longarm slowed his horse, put him into a walk, and then came up beside Virgil and stopped.

He said, "What are you doing this afternoon, Virgil?"

The blank-eyed young man looked up at him. He said, "Waitin' my daddy. My bubbas."

Longarm said, "Your daddy and your bubbas ain't gonna be coming home anytime soon."

Virgil had a skinning knife in his right hand. He drew figures in the dust with the point of it. He said as if he had studied on it, "Who taken my daddy, my bubbas? Who got 'em?"

Longarm said, "The long knives, Virgil. The long knives." He watched the boy carefully.

Virgil looked up at him. "The yellow legs? Them blue bellies?"

Longarm said slowly, "Yeah. The soldiers. The long knives. They've got your daddy and your brothers."

Virgil stood up. Only then could Longarm see that on the other side of him was a skinned rabbit. He thought, well, so much for Mr. Castle's theory that Virgil liked bunny rabbits. He turned his horse out to the main part of the road.

He asked, "Virgil, can you shoot a rifle?"

Virgil stared at him blankly.

He asked again, "Virgil, can you shoot a big rifle?"

Virgil said, "Long knives got my daddy. Got my brothers."

Longarm just nodded and kicked his chestnut into a lope. He thought he better have a real quick talk with Mr. Castle.

But as he circled around the fort and came even with Clell Martin's little shack, he could see the old man out in front of his porch. On a whim, he slowed the chestnut and turned in and rode toward the old man.

Clell Martin was feeding chickens, scattering shelled corn out for them beside his house near a chicken run. Longarm pulled up his chestnut and waited until Martin finished.

Martin put down his feed bucket and came through the screen gate, shutting it behind him. He dusted off his hands.

He said, "Hi there, young man. Step down and have yourself a cup of coffee with me."

Longarm dismounted but he said, "Well, much obliged for the offer of coffee, Mr. Martin, but I am heading on back into town. Wouldn't mind sitting out here on the porch and visiting a few minutes, though. You care for a smoke?"

Clell Martin waved away the offer. "Never took to tobacco that away. Always chewed it."

"Well, some smoke it and some chew it."

Martin said, "I tell you, back during the War of the Confederacy, there was many a night when that chaw of tobacco was my best friend out there on guard duty out near them Yankee lines."

They sat down on the porch. Longarm got his cheroot lit and then shoved his hat back. He said, "Mr. Martin, you don't like the Castles just some little bit, do ya?"

Clell Martin immediately got agitated. "Well, if they were to all drown or be burned in Hell's fire, wouldn't make no difference to me. And I guarantee you that if they drown, they will be dried out in Hell."

Longarm said, "What about Virgil? What do you think about Virgil?" His thinking was that maybe Mr. Martin had seen Virgil lurking about the road near the fort late at night. Of course, an old man like Mr. Martin more than likely went to sleep early.

Mr. Martin's response surprised him. He said, "Virgil? Why, Virgil ain't no damn Castle. Where did you get that idea? Virgil is an Injun. He was taken up by them damn Castles when he was just a kid. He ain't no damn one of them."

Longarm said, "A blue-eyed Indian?"

"That don't make no difference," Martin said. "That man is a Comanche Indian. Ain't you never noticed him around? Why, he is sly as a fox—that man can outrun a deer. That man is a Comanche brave. Why, that man and I have had some good talks. A lot of folks thinks he's a little slow, but that ain't so. It's just that he don't speak the lingo as much as you might want him to. He keeps pretty much to himself and he keeps his thinking to himself. He don't like them blue bellies any better than I do and you can imagine why. I figure them yellow legs killed his folks and the Castles drug him off with them."

Longarm gazed at the man in disbelief. He said, "He's blue-eyed. He's got light-colored hair. He's light-complected."

Martin spit tobacco juice in the dust. "Don't make no never mind. You've got your different kinds of Injuns. It's what's inside a man that makes him an Injun. Virgil—and that ain't his real name by the way, his real name is Running Wolf."

"Did he tell you that?"

Martin spit again. "Didn't need to. I knowed it the minute I talked to him. I said, I reckon your name is Running Wolf, ain't it?"

"And he said yes?"

"He ain't never said no and he'll damn sure answer to it when you call him that. Naw, naw, don't be confusing him with them damn Castles. He's a good man."

"I see," Longarm said uneasily. "Well, I guess I had better be getting on back to town, Mr. Martin. Maybe you and I could talk again sometime."

Clell Martin walked out to his horse with him. As Longarm put his foot into his stirrup and mounted, Martin said, "Well, I don't know what is comin' to this country, but I tell you, I'm about ready to see a better class of people comin' around. If we don't get rid of that bunch doing what they call Reconstruction, this country ain't ever going to do right by itself."

Longarm looked down at the man and nodded his head.

He turned his horse and rode thoughtfully down the road that would take him back into town and to the jail.

He almost didn't go to the jail when he got into town. He was tired and disgusted and wanted a drink and some time to himself. He also didn't want to listen to any more of Mr. Vernon Castle's outraged protests or to be called a sonofabitch twenty or thirty times more. But in the end, the prospect of informing Mr. Vernon Castle that, yes indeed, his son Virgil Castle did like bunny rabbits, especially skinned bunny rabbits, proved too strong a lure to pass up.

He turned his horse in at the hotel stable and then walked across to Sheriff Smith's office. His spurs jingled as he stepped up on the boardwalk. He turned the knob and then swung the door open wide and stopped in amazement at what he saw. There was Vernon Castle and his two sons and the sheriff and Clarence Botts, all in the outer office. The sheriff was busy getting the gunbelts of the two younger men.

Longarm said, "What the hell is going on here?"

They all glanced up, surprise on their faces.

It was Mr. Botts who did the answering. He came toward Longarm waving a piece of paper in his hand. He said, "Just take a look at this, Deputy Marshal Long. You'll see this is an authentic notice from the federal judge in San Antonio vacating your bench warrant for the arrest of my clients. It is a habeas corpus notification, and you are hereby ordered by Judge Fisher in San Antonio to release my clients."

Longarm took the paper and studied it for a moment. It was a handwritten document on plain stationery bearing no stamp or any official heading. He looked up at Botts.

"This doesn't look authentic to me," he said. "In fact, this looks like something you might have written yourself in the hotel."

Botts swelled himself up, which was difficult for a man of his small stature. "By God, sir," he said. "That document was handwritten by Judge Fisher and signed by his own hand. I found the man at his home at night. There were no official papers to be had, and I was in a hurry to catch a train to return here so that I could relieve my clients of this durance vile that you have subjected them to."

Longarm read the document quickly. The wording sounded official, and he knew that there was a Judge Fisher in San Antonio who was a federal judge, but he was not inclined to release the Castles and he was going to grasp at any reason he could find. He shook his head. "Makes no difference. This is not an official document as far as I'm concerned. So, gentlemen, you can just head right on back into those cells."

Vernon Castle had been standing by the sheriff's desk. He stepped out sideways. He said, "Marshal, you can go to hell, you sonofabitch. That release was duly and authentically obtained and you, by God, will abide by its authenticity. What document did you have? You had a telegram. This, at least, is in the judge's own handwriting."

Longarm said, "Well, I don't know about that, Mr. Castle. I'm afraid I'll be forced to put ya'll back in those cells until I can get this verified."

Vernon Castle said with some heat, "Like hell you will."

Longarm's eyes suddenly shifted to Glenn and his brother Billy Bob. They had their hands dangerously close to the gunbelts that were lying on the sheriff's desk. He said, "You two, back up there. Back up right now. Either one of you reaches his hands toward one of those guns and I'm gonna put a hole in you. You understand?"

Sheriff Smith said, "Now, damnit, Long. I've had about enough of you. You get the hell out of my jail and stay out. These men have been released and I'm going to release them. I consider that bench warrant vacated by the paper that Lawyer Botts has brought from San Antonio. That's good enough for me and it's going to be damn well be good enough for you."

Longarm said, "Fine then. I am now officially charging you, Vernon Castle, and you, Glenn Castle, and you Billy Bob Castle with conspiracy in the murder of five United States Cavalry soldiers from Fort Concho. So turn around and march back in to those cells."

The sheriff came around his desk and stood between the Castles and Longarm. "Not by a damn sight, you're not," he said. "Murder is a local matter, and you damn well won't be throwing your federal weight around in here on that. I can assure you of that, Marshal."

Longarm said, "Well, that might be so, Sheriff Smith. However, in this case, the murdered parties were federal soldiers, and that makes it a federal case and my jurisdiction overrides you. Now get the hell out of the way so I can put these men back in their cells."

The sheriff stood his ground. He said in a cold voice, "Listen, Long. You've rode roughshod over me about as long as I'm gonna stand for it. Now you get out of my office and you stay out of my office. You ain't welcome in this jail anymore and you're not going to use it for your personal lockup. I don't care if you are a federal deputy marshal." He put his hand near the butt of his revolver. It was not quite a threatening gesture, but it had implications.

Without pause, Longarm drew his revolver and thumbed the hammer back. It made a loud *clitch-clatch* in the room. The noise startled Clarence Botts. He stepped back several paces. Longarm said, "Now, I'm only going to say this once, Sheriff. You either stay out of this, or I'm going to put you in one of those cells with these men. You are interfering with a federal officer in the performance of his duty and that is a felony, and I will damn well put you in jail and bring you to trial for it. Do you understand me?"

The sheriff took a step backwards. The move seemed to unite him with the three Castles, who were standing near the lockup door. Then the sheriff said, "You're cutting it mighty thin, Long, mighty thin. I don't think you want the trouble you are fixing to get."

Longarm said evenly, "Smith, with your left hand reach around and unbuckle your gunbelt. Let it fall to the floor."

The sheriff stared at him. He said, "You're disarming me in my own jail?"

"I am disarming a man who is trying to interfere with a federal officer. The fact that you're the sheriff don't cut no ice with me. Now, unbuckle that gunbelt and let it fall to the floor or I'm going to have to make use of this revolver in my hand."

Vernon Castle said, "You wouldn't dare shoot."

With his eyes still on the sheriff, Longarm said, "Do you want to bet your life on that, or bet your sons' lives on that, or do you want to bet the sheriff's life on that?" He reached up and tapped the badge on his chest. "You might defy Custis Long the man and get away with it, but you damn well ain't going to defy this. This says I'm a deputy United States marshal and that I represent the federal government. You're not going to defy that. Now, I'm not even going to count to three, but if I don't see some action here right quick, this revolver is going to go off. Is that clear?"

The sheriff's face paled. "Now wait a minute. Hold on. Hold on there, Long. Let's talk about this for a minute."

"The only talk I want to hear is either you taking that gunbelt off and getting in that jail, or giving me your word that you are not going to interfere with me anymore."

The sheriff said, his voice unsteady, "Look. You can't do this to a man in his own town. It ain't fittin'. We're both law officers."

"That's true. Why don't you try acting like one?"

"You have the right to lock them up on a federal charge for conspiracy to murder?"

"In my opinion I do. If I don't, then I'm the one that has to pay for it, do you understand? The responsibility is mine, but if you interfere with me, the responsibility is yours. Even if I shoot you, the responsibility is yours."

The sheriff turned to the Castles and said in an uncertain voice, "Mr. Castle, I don't seem to have much choice here. I'm mighty sorry about this, but he is a federal marshal, and if he says that he has jurisdiction, there ain't a hell of a lot that I can say about it."

Vernon Castle stared at Longarm with hate and venom in his eyes. "Don't worry about it, Smith," he said. "I don't expect you to stand up to this bully, but by God, his day is coming. You can depend on that."

Longarm said, "If I'm wrong, you'll have no problems giving me enough trouble to last me a lifetime. But I don't think I'm wrong and I don't think that you're going to be able to get my badge and I don't think that you're going to be able to get out of that jail. Now, when you settle down and are willing to talk some sense to me, I might consider letting you out of that jail, but not until then. Now, all three of you turn around, march back through that lockup door, and get back to your cells. And Sheriff, you follow right along behind them and make sure they do."

As Longarm was about to step forward, the lawyer said in a trembling voice, "What am I supposed to do now? How can I get them released?"

Longarm gave him a glance. He said, "Well, Mr. Botts, I guess you're going to have to go back to San Antonio and see Judge Fisher again." Longarm handed him the document he'd brought back from San Antonio. "Here, take this with you. Maybe the judge can write a new writ of habeas corpus on the back and save the government some paper."

He followed along as the sheriff took the three Castles and put them back into their original cells. Vernon Castle was almost shaking with rage, and his two sons were no less angry.

As the sheriff passed Longarm in the corridor between the cells, he muttered, "Well, I hope you're happy, Longarm. You've made me look like a piss-pot fool in this town."

"On the contrary," Longarm said. "I forced you to do your job. That ought to make you a big man. You stood up to me, didn't you?"

The sheriff said, "Oh, go to hell, you sonofabitch."

Longarm shook his head. "I do not believe I have ever been called a sonofabitch more times in as short a time in all my life." With that, he found a chair and pulled it up in front of Mr. Castle's cell. "Now, Vernon. I'm going to sit right down here and you and I are going to talk. Right now you don't want to talk, and maybe you're not going to want to talk for an hour or two hours or three hours or six hours, but I am going to sit here until you are ready to talk to me. Then we're going to see if maybe we can't work something out about this matter."

Vernon Castle gave him a look. "You go straight to hell," he said. "None of my sons have had anything to do with the murder of soldiers."

Longarm said, "But you don't know that, Mr. Castle, you don't know that about Virgil. Now, I'm going to want all the information I can get from you about Virgil. I'm going to try and reach an agreement with you about Virgil. I think that maybe there is something that we can do about him and if you're willing to do it, ya'll can all get out of jail and we can all take care of Virgil without hurting him."

Vernon Castle said, "Yeah, what?"

Longarm hitched his chair closer to the cell door. "Well, there's more ways to kill a cat than to choke him to death with butter. Right now we've got a situation that needs some long, hard thought and you are going to have to be willing to cooperate with me."

Vernon Castle said, "I'm listening, but I doubt there is anything that you can say that would interest me very much."

Longarm said, "I take it then, sir, that you like it in that jail cell?"

Vernon Castle stared back at him.

Longarm said, "Because I can assure you that, one way or another, I am going to keep you and those two sons of yours in these jail cells until I get to the bottom of this matter. And I'll tell you the reason for that. You see, I don't like San Angelo. I don't like being here, but I can't leave here until I get this matter settled. So I don't give a damn how uncomfortable, how undignified, how embarrassed you and your boys are. I'm going to keep you in these damn cells on one pretext or another until you give me some cooperation. Is that understood, Mr. Castle?"

Vernon Castle stared straight back at him. "You think that you're a mighty big man, don't you, Long?"

From the other cell, Longarm was amazed to hear Glenn say, "Pa, why don't you listen to him. For God's sake, we've got to get out of this damn place. My leg is itching. I'm disgusted with this whole affair. You know as well as I do you can't keep tabs on Virgil every minute, so you don't know what he's been up to."

Vernon Castle said angrily over Longarm's shoulder, "Shut your mouth, Glenn. Shut your mouth right now."

There came a rumbling voice. It was Billy Bob. He said, "Pa, maybe Glenn's right."

Longarm looked at the elder Castle. He said, "Well, Vernon, are you ready to talk turkey yet—or Injun, I should say? What'll it be? A little cooperation or a lot of jail time?"

Vernon Castle looked down at the floor. Longarm could see the stubbornness in the bow of his neck. He didn't think that he was going to give in easy.

Chapter 10

He spent a long two hours with Castle. When he left the jail, he didn't know whether to be angry, puzzled, or amused. What the man had told him simply didn't sound like the reasoning of a businessman. When Longarm had suggested that there were other methods of getting the garrison to either move or cooperate, Mr. Castle's answer had been simple: that would have allowed everyone else in on his good thing.

His good thing.

That was what Longarm thought about as he walked back to the Cutler House and went to his room. He was tired. He wasn't a man who liked to get off his schedule as much as he had been off the past five days. He was way short on his sleep, and his eating and drinking habits hadn't improved either. He decided that he would lie down and have a good rest before going out around midnight and making the circle one last time. He had a lot on his mind, so before he lay down, he poured himself another glass of Maryland whiskey and sat down on the bed and thought.

He wondered if Virgil was truly capable of bushwhacking the soldiers with the type of weaponry that had been involved. True, Longarm, in his reconnaissance of the house, had found plenty of heavy rifles and plenty of ammunition. But he wondered if Virgil in his simplemindedness was capable of that kind of action. Running across the plains and chasing a deer on foot, or skinning a rabbit or cutting a steak off a horse, seemed more in his line of work. But skulking up a butte and lying in wait and then using a fairly complex rifle just didn't seem to fit in with the boy.

Boy, he thought. Well, he was a boy in many ways, even though as a man he was fully grown.

But there just didn't seem to be anyone else. At first, he had liked Clell Martin as the prime suspect, but he had a hard time visualizing the crippled-up old man getting about the country that deftly. At least two of those shots had been fired from a higher elevation, and that meant the old man would have had to climb a butte. Longarm wondered if the old man could do that with his hip. And also, one of the soldiers had been killed on the south road, and that was a good ten or twelve miles from Martin's home. It would have taken some scrambling on his part to have gotten there riding cross-country on a horse or a mule. Longarm assumed that he had a mule, since that was all that he'd seen about the place.

But then, it all sounded crazy to begin with. Martin didn't even realize that Reconstruction was over with. He had the hatred for the Yankees that many Confederate veterans did, but then there weren't many Confederate veterans murdering Yankee soldiers. He doubted very seriously that Virgil thought of himself as an avenging Indian. The best idea that he had come up with was that

Virgil had overheard his father expressing displeasure with the garrison and had acted out of love and loyalty to his family. That was the only thing that made sense.

Finally Longarm sighed and started to strip down to get a good long nap. It was all too much. He had come very close to striking a bargain with Mr. Castle. In return for Longarm releasing him and Billy Bob and Glenn, Castle had indicated he might be willing to commit Virgil to an insane asylum.

Longarm didn't know if that would do the trick or not. It could be that Virgil wasn't really the killer and that the killing would go on. It could be that Virgil really wasn't dangerous at all, and then it would do him a tremendous disservice to shut him up inside cold concrete walls. Longarm had never seen the inside of an insane asylum, but he had heard stories. He didn't think that it was the most festive place to spend one's days.

He finally gave up the whole job of thinking as a bad endeavor. He finished his whiskey, and then shucked off the last of his clothes and lay down on the bed. He was plenty tired. It felt good to close his eyes and relax. Before he knew it, he wasn't aware of any trouble at all.

He came awake sometime later to the sound of loud pounding at his door. At first, he was groggy and couldn't locate himself. The room was dark and it was dark outside the window. When he could finally gather his wits, he swung around on his bed and lit the lamp, yawning for a moment, before he called out, "All right! All right! I'm coming! Dammit, I'm coming!" He didn't know if they could hear him or not, but they were damn sure going to have to wait.

He pulled on his jeans, not bothering with his boots, and with his revolver in his hand went to the door. He said without opening it, "Who is it? What do you want?"

A muffled voice said, "It's Sergeant McClellan, sir. I've come from the fort. I've come from the commander."

Longarm quickly unlocked the door and pulled it back. A trooper stood there in the hall. He looked agitated.

Longarm said, "What the hell is going on? What time is it?"

The trooper said, "Sir. The fort is under fire. We're being sniped at. It's twelve-fifteen or twelve-thirty. The captain said that we weren't supposed to do anything, that I was supposed to come get you. He said it was a civilian matter. I've lost time trying to circle around the sniper. Yes, sir, it's twelve-thirty."

Longarm said, "All right, Sergeant. Calm down. You come on back in here with me while I get dressed and tell me what you know about it."

They went back into the bedroom. Longarm got the rest of his clothes on and pulled on his boots and checked his derringer, revolver, and rifle while the sergeant told him of the events.

The sergeant said that since about eleven-fifteen or so, the compound had been under attack from rifle fire. There had been single shots, sometimes fired a minute apart, sometimes faster, sometimes slower.

Longarm said, "Anybody hurt? Anybody killed?"

Sergeant McClellan said, "Some of the boys have been hit by flying splinters of glass and pieces of roof when them big-ass shells came blasting through the barracks. Then Johnny Whitley was hit in the arm. The surgeon reckons it broke the bone. That's a big shell! We figure

160

there's four or five horses dead. It ain't been going on all that long. Like I say, it started, we reckon . . . well, it's . . . it took me twenty minutes to get into town, so I guess we were under attack for about forty-five minutes before Captain Montrose sent me for you."

Longarm said, "Can you tell where the fire is coming from?"

"Yes, sir, it's coming off a butte a little to the north and west of the fort. Appears to be about a half a mile away. We can see the muzzle flashes."

Longarm said, "Can you tell if it's more than one shooter or not?"

The sergeant scratched his head under his garrison cap. He said, "Well, sir, that do be hard to say. He's moving around. He ain't staying in one position. Or *they* are moving around and ain't staying in one position. But we never saw two muzzle flashes at one time, leastwise nobody thought to say anything about it if they did. I mean, well, I don't know. We was just kind of figuring on it being one feller, but there could be two, I guess. I don't know."

Longarm said, "Well, Sergeant, we're damn sure not gonna find out standing around here. You head on back to the fort and tell the captain that I'm on the job."

The sergeant said, "Don't you need me to show you where the shooter is?"

Longarm said dryly, "For some reason I think I'm going to be able to figure it out."

He and the sergeant left together. Outside the hotel, Todd ran to fetch Longarm's horse while the sergeant rode away.

When Todd brought his horse back, the young man looked anxious and excited. He said, "There's trouble, ain't there, Mr. Long? I mean, Marshal Long. I mean, you sure fooled me about that."

"Yes, Todd, I know. Yes, there is trouble."

"Who's a-doin it?"

Longarm swung up into the saddle. He said, "I think I'm finally going to find out."

He rode out of town northeast toward the fort. He had the feeling he sometimes got when he knew he was about to finally get to the nub of a matter. He felt like he was fixing to be able to scratch the itch that had been driving him crazy for more than a week. He rode swiftly as long as he was on the road, making good time for better than two miles. As the road swung east and toward the fort, he slowed the chestnut and started him into the thick brush and heavy going of the sand, rocks, and cactus. He pulled the horse down to a walk, but it was still hard on the animal. Occasionally he would stumble and Longarm would have to keep him afoot by the deft use of the reins. It was almost a moonless night. There was just the tiniest sliver of pale yellow in the eastern sky. High clouds in the dark sky overhead occasionally drifted past.

He picked his way carefully, heading in the general direction of the fort. He was not definitely certain where he was going but he had a fair idea. After about thirty minutes of careful traveling, he passed Clell Martin's shack to his right. Not long after that, he began to hear the sound of a distant rifle. It sounded like thunder from way across the valley. There was an echo to it.

He finally hit a cleared space and was able to urge his horse to greater speed. He had left the road because he had a fair idea where the rifleman was firing from and he wanted to be able to come up on him from the rear. He went on for approximately another half mile and then dismounted, taking his rifle from the saddle boot.

He paused a moment to make sure he had extra shells in his shirt pocket that would fit both his rifle and his .44 revolver. He felt inside his belt buckle to make sure the derringer hadn't slipped out in the rough ride.

He tied the chestnut to a mesquite tree and started forward, having rough going in his high-heel boots through the sand and the rocks. Now, of course, the firing was much nearer. He could see the butte where he knew it was coming from outlined in front of him in the dim sky. It was not particularly high, perhaps two hundred feet, but it was broad and squat. It was going to be easy to climb—easy, that is, if he didn't have to do it under fire.

He considered taking off his boots to make the climbing easier, but he knew his stocking feet couldn't take it for five minutes over the rough terrain. He took his hat off and laid it carefully on a rock so he'd be sure and find it on his way back to his horse. That hat had cost quite a bit of money and he had no intention of losing it in the apprehension of a crazy man.

He slowly started climbing. In the light and with the proper shoes and without being encumbered by the rifle, it would have been easy going, even if there had been a killer at the top. But under the conditions, he made slow progress. He counted five shots fired by the time he managed to make it within ten yards of the flat top that was littered with boulders. He knew that somewhere on that flat top of the butte, behind one of those boulders, crouched a man with a long-range, heavy-caliber rifle who was carrying out an insane plan.

The question in his mind was how much leeway should you give a man like that. Do you ask a crazy man to surrender? Does a crazy man even understand what it means to surrender? If you have a man doing something wrong, but he doesn't think it's wrong, how do you appeal to his sense of guilt? You can't say, "Stop doing that, it's wrong. I've come to arrest you." It was a perplexing question that he wasn't sure he'd ever faced before. Always before, the men he'd gone up against had known what they were doing. They were outlaws, they were criminals, they were killers, they were robbers. But the man who was now only a few yards away from him thought that what he was doing was perfectly right. However, that was not going to make it any less dangerous to try to arrest him rather than kill him. The easiest thing would be to kill the man outright, but Longarm couldn't bring himself to do that. He was going to have to somehow talk the man into disarming himself. It was going to be quite a little problem. He did not want to shoot unless he was forced to. To him it would be like killing a child.

He had worked his way as close as he could without making a move. He heard the rifle boom one more time, sounding like a cannon at such close quarters. He stepped out from behind the boulder and said, "Well, don't you think that's enough?" In the faint moonlight, the figure turned and Longarm almost stepped back in surprise.

It was Clell Martin.

In his hands was a long Springfield .58-caliber cap-and-ball percussion rifle. He had just fired it. It was now empty and it would take it thirty seconds to reload.

In spite of himself, Longarm said, "Mr. Martin. My God, sir. What are you doing?"

The old man peered into the dimness, and even though Longarm was standing only a few feet away, it took him some time to recognize the marshal. He said, "Be that you, Mr. Long?"

Longarm said, "Yes." He slowly brought his own rifle up to bear. "Clell, put that rifle down. I know it's not loaded anymore. I know it's a single-shot, but put it down anyway."

Clell Martin looked puzzled. He said, "What's all the fuss about? Damn carpetbaggers are a-ruinin' this country. What you wanna stop me for? Ain't it about time they went back up north?"

Longarm said softly, "Clell, Reconstruction has been over for years. Those are just garrison troops training for the Indian wars west of here, out in New Mexico."

Clell Martin was still holding the Springfield. He squinted his eyes. He said, "Why, you sonofabitch. You've been a spy right along, ain't you? You've been a-spying on me for them bastards. Don't you know, boy, that Reconstruction is ruining the South? We'll never come back as long as we leave them sonofabitches down here. Ain't it enough they whipped us in the war? Do they have to humiliate us the rest of our lives?"

Longarm took a slow step forward. He said, "Clell, have you been shooting those soldiers along the road?"

Clell Martin gave him a defiant look. "You ain't never been in a war, have ya, boy? I bet you never, ever seen a calvary charge, have ya, boy?"

Longarm nodded. "I have. But right here and now is not the time or place to talk about it. Let's you and me go on down, maybe go over to your cabin and discuss it. Right now, I want you to put that rifle down. I note that you have a revolver stuck in your waistband. I want you to get rid of that too."

Clell Martin said, "I ain't doin' nothin' with you, you scalawag. You're a damn . . . I don't know if you're a scalawag or a carpetbagger. You come along and cozy up to me and try to make friends, and all the time you was a spying on me, wasn't you? You were scouting me out, weren't you? By God, you're from that fort, ain't ya? You know, seems to me that I noticed you went out to that fort more than several times. And you had you that story about them horses. Just who are you, mister?"

Longarm tapped the badge. He knew it was hard to see in the light. "Clell, I'm a deputy United States marshal and I am going to have to get you to come off the top of this butte with me so we can sit down and have a talk. Now, put your weapon down now."

Without making a threat of it, he raised his rifle and brought it to bear on Clell's chest. He said, "Let's don't make this any harder than it has to be, Mr. Martin."

At that instant he heard a wild yell, a sound he had heard before. As a heavy figure stuck him from behind and above, he fell trying to remember where. As his face ground into the gritty dirt of the butte top, he remembered that it had been in the parlor of the Castle house. He could feel Virgil's strong arms grappling around him, pinning his own arms. He fought him as best as he could.

As he fell, he could hear Martin yelling, "Get him, Injun. Get him, Injun, get him."

He jabbed backward with an elbow and felt the grip around his neck loosen. He kicked out, connecting solidly with a shin, and felt the grip loosen even more. But then he felt a hand near his sidearm and he whirled, trying to get his right side to the ground, trying to keep his revolver

166

from being taken from him. Now he had Virgil almost in front of him. He was surprised just how incredibly strong the slimly built young man was, but then he supposed that if a man spent his life bounding across the pastures and bounding up and down the buttes, he probably got made into rawhide and barbed wire.

Virgil went for his throat hold again, but Longarm knocked his hands loose and then got his own hand under Virgil's chin and shoved. Then he was able to draw his right leg up and catch the man in the midsection with his boot heel. Virgil gave a grunt. Longarm shoved and sent him sprawling. Longarm came struggling to his feet moving as rapidly as he could, but he was too late.

Virgil had landed a few feet away, but Martin was standing solidly planted in front of Longarm, an old Colt revolver steady in his right hand. The old man said, "Just you hold it right there, mister, just hold it right there. Don't you make no sudden moves."

Longarm was winded from his struggles with Virgil. He let his right arm drift past his holster. He could tell that his revolver had been dislodged, and of course he had lost his rifle in the struggle. Now, except for the derringer, he was disarmed.

Virgil had gotten to his feet. He was wearing his breech-cloth, and his long stringy hair was wild and dirty. His face bore a childish imitation of war paint. In his right hand, he now held a long skinning knife.

Martin said, "That Injun got ya, didn't he? Mr. Deputy Marshal carpetbaggin' sonofabitch. How'd ya like that Injun getting ya? You wasn't expectin' that, was ya?"

Longarm said calmly, "Mr. Martin, he's not an Indian. His name is Virgil Castle. He is the son of a white man. He's a white man."

Virgil Castle spoke. "Long knives take my daddy. Clell, this long knife? He long knife? He no got blue-belly suit."

Clell Martin licked his lips. He said, "That's right, Running Wolf. He's a long knife, just sure as shootin'. Never mind about the uniform, he just ain't got it on, but he's a long knife just the same. How you want to finish him off? You want to scalp him alive?"

Longarm said, more to satisfy his own curiosity than anything else, "I see how you did it now. You both did it. Virgil shot the trooper on the south road and you shot the troopers on the north. Isn't that right, Clell?"

"What you know and what you hear ain't never gonna be told, so it don't make a damn. Besides, we're mighty proud of what we've done."

Virgil Castle said, "My daddy hates them blue bellies. My daddy wants them blue bellies to leave. I want to please my daddy. I killed them blue bellies."

Clell Martin said, "You damn right you did, Running Wolf. You done real good."

Virgil Castle asked, "This blue belly? This man blue belly?"

Clell Martin said, "Yeah, Running Wolf. He's a blue belly. He may be the worst blue belly of all of them. You want him with your knife like you did the one in the alley?"

Longarm said, "So you killed all six?"

Clell Martin said, "It's fixin' to be seven."

Longarm asked, "Can you spare me a few minutes, Mr. Martin? If you are intent on killing me, the least you can do would be to tell me why you went about it and how you went about it. I mean, I'm kinda curious. I mean, I'm the one that's come out on this black night. I'm the one that came up here. Mr. Martin, you forget that I could have shot you while you were leaning over that rock firing on the fort and I didn't do it. So I think the least you owe me is an explanation."

All the while he was talking, Longarm had hung both thumbs in his gunbelt. His right thumb was very carefully working the handle of his derringer up into the palm of his hand. It was going to be a poor weapon in the dark and at the three- or four-yard range that the two men faced him from, but it was the only weapon that he had left.

He said, "It seems to me it's the least you could do for a man you are considering killing. And by the way, I am not a Yankee. I'm from Colorado. I never had anything to do with the Civil War."

Clell Martin exploded. He said, "Goddammit, don't call it the Civil War, you Yankee sonofabitch. It was the War of the Confederacy. Any fool knows that."

Longarm said placatingly, "All right, all right, all right. The War of the Confederacy. But will you still tell me about the soldiers here? Tell me why Virgil did what he did? I think I understand why you did what you did."

Martin looked undecided. He glanced over at Virgil, then said, "Well, maybe I owe you that much for not backshooting me, which is what most Yankee dogs would have done."

For about three minutes, he sketched out the murders that had occurred over a two-month period. He ended by saying, "And now you are going to be the last. I am fixin' to set this Indian loose on you. How do you want to do it, Running Wolf? Do you want to just skin him alive, or do you want to take him straight in the belly, Running Wolf? Remember, this is the long knife that put your daddy in jail. Matter of fact, I have it on mighty good authority that he is the one that done it. He's done the same as admit it to me. He's the marshal. He's the worst of the long knives. In fact, he may have already kilt your daddy."

By now, Longarm had worked the derringer up so that he had it concealed in the palm of his right hand. At the words from Clell Martin about killing his daddy, Virgil Castle began a low growl in his throat. His head came down and his arms went out from his sides. The skinning knife was in his right hand. He began making animal noises.

Clell Martin said, "Go get him, Indian. Go get him, Running Wolf, he's yo'rn."

Longarm had his back pressed up against a boulder. He didn't want to take the rush of the young man with no room to give, so as Virgil Castle started toward him, he stepped forward, hoping to be able to catch the wildly swinging knife arm in his left hand. They came together a yard from where Longarm had been standing. Longarm missed his grab at the arm. He felt the knife slice into his left bicep. He didn't know how deep he was cut. All he knew was that, regretfully, he had no choice. He had the derringer pressed right against the breastbone of the young man.

He pulled the trigger. There was a loud explosion and the young man slumped.

As quickly as he could, Longarm grabbed him under the arms despite his own wounded arm, holding him up as protection from the shot that Clell Martin fired from his Navy Colt. The shot took Virgil Castle in the back. It saved Longarm's life. Longarm had his right arm stretched under the dead young man's armpit. It was a long shot in the gloomy darkness, but he fired straight at Clell Martin. The .38 slug hit him in the chest.

For a second nothing happened except that Clell Martin got a surprised look on his face. Then the Colt fell from his fingers and dropped to the ground. For a moment, he just stood there and then, very slowly, he crumpled.

With a sigh, Longarm let the body of Virgil Castle slide to the ground. Before he did anything else, he searched the ground and quickly found his .44 revolver. The two-shot derringer was all used up.

Keeping the revolver pointed at Clell Martin, he went over to the old man. He stood over him. It was difficult to see in the dark so he nudged him with the toe of his boot. Martin didn't move. Longarm reached down and felt his heart. His hand came away sticky with blood. He wiped it on the old man's shirt. He was dead.

He got up and slowly moved around the top of the butte until he located his rifle. Holding it straight up, he fired three quick shots into the air. He paused, then fired three quick additional shots. It was the traditional close-on-me signal of the cavalry.

After that, he went over and slumped down on a rock next to the body of Clell Martin. He felt very drained and very sad. He could feel the blood from the knife slash trickling down his left arm. He didn't think it was very bad. He flexed it a few times and it seemed to work all right. Apparently his muscles hadn't been cut across, just sliced downward. It was, he thought, a shame, a damn shame. Eight men were dead. Eight men had died because of one man's greed, one man's confusion, and another man's revengeful insanity. It was a sad commentary on the whole state of affairs.

While he waited for the soldiers to arrive to pick up the bodies, and to make his report to Captain Montrose, he sat and tried to think good thoughts about Mabelle Russell.

Maybe he could even stick around long enough to pay her one more visit. Maybe they could even have another nice dinner together. Hell, it was something pleasant to think about—something other than the slaughter on top of a butte. He was not proud of what he'd done, but it had been what he'd had to do. He'd never been given any choice.

He sat there, studying the night, noting the lack of stars, waiting for the soldiers from the fort to arrive. Then he got up and walked partway down the butte, if for no other reason than to get away from the bodies of Clell Martin and Virgil Castle. Normally bodies didn't bother him, but this time they did. He felt as if he had killed men who deserved help rather than killing. And he wished there had been something he could have done other than what he had been forced to.

He got out a cheroot and lit it, the flame of the match bursting bright in the dark night. The only good that he could see coming of the matter was that now he could go home. There was little doubt in his mind that the two, in some sort of strange partnership, had been the murderers of the six soldiers.

In reality, he couldn't actually take credit for flushing them out. They had flushed themselves out. He supposed that they had begun firing at the fort out of frustration because the soldiers, out of fear, had quit frequenting the road to town at night. That meant, in the end, it had been the soldiers' fear itself that had solved the mystery. The only thing he could be grateful for was that no one else had been killed in this last attack. The worst thing that could have happened would have been if Clell and Virgil had been able to restrain themselves for a time until the fear had worn off and the soldiers had fallen back into their pattern of nightly trips into town. Then the pair would have had targets aplenty.

But he supposed that you couldn't expect patience from a man who thought he was an Indian and another who thought that Reconstruction was still going on. It was a sad state of affairs all around. He knew that the captain would thank him. He knew that Vernon Castle would curse him. He knew that the sheriff would probably file a written complaint against him. He knew that Vernon Castle, through his lawyer, would no doubt file a civil action against him. But in the end, it just came down to doing the job that the badge said you had to do. Nowhere in his rules of conduct was it specified that it was supposed to be fun or even pleasant. Nowhere was he guaranteed anything more than long hours, poor pay, and lonely work. Well, he decided, if in the end there were more people happy with your work than unhappy, then you'd done a good job. He reckoned, judging it that way, that his time in San Angelo had not been misspent.

Chapter 11

It was five days later and Longarm was sitting across the desk from Billy Vail in Billy's office in Denver. Billy had just finished reading Longarm's report and was glancing at it again.

Finally he threw it on the desk and said, "Hell, Custis. That may be the shortest damn report ever filed in the history of this office. There is a world of story behind a few of those statements you made in there."

Longarm said, "Such as what?"

Billy picked the paper up again. "Well, just for openers, right here you start this thing out by saying that due to the greed of one individual, Vernon Castle, six troopers of the United States Cavalry stationed at Fort Concho, San Angelo, Texas, were mistakenly killed by a misguided ex-Confederate soldier and a simpleminded young man who had been convinced that he was an Indian. What greed? What greed, Custis, are you talking about?"

Longarm shifted uncomfortably in his chair. He said, "I didn't really want to put it in an official report, Billy, because it sounds so damn silly. I mean, you take the consequences that came about because of what Vernon Castle had in his mind and what he was trying do, well, it's a damn shame. I hated to put it down."

"Well, you can just damn well tell me and let me be the judge of whether you put it down or not."

Longarm said, "Well, Vernon Castle thought that there was a spring that was very near the surface right under Fort Concho. He'd got hold of a dowser—you know, a water witch."

Billy Vail said, "You mean one of them kind that goes around with a willow stick and when the water pulls at it, it pulls toward the ground?"

Longarm nodded. "Exactly."

Billy Vail said, "Well, you know, I've heard of that working."

Longarm said, "And I've heard of it not working also. But the point of it is that this dowser, the water witch that Vernon Castle had brought in to try to find some water near the surface in that dry-as-a-bone part of the country, had got onto to what he claimed was an underground stream. He followed it straight through Fort Concho. He said it came to no more than five or six feet below the surface there, and said that it could be dug up in one afternoon except that the soldiers had a camp there. They had a fort there. It was government land, and that was what caused Vernon Castle to set into doing what he did."

"You mean, trying to get that garrison moved?"

"That's right. So you see how silly that would have looked in an official report. A rancher tries to get an army garrison moved because he believes there is water under the fort. I'm not going to write that. Somebody is liable to find it ten years from now and wonder if maybe there wasn't another crazy person involved in the case."

Billy rubbed his face. "Why didn't they just go to the commander of that fort, Captain—uh, what's his name, Captain Montrose—and ask him if they could dig for water?"

Longarm sat back in his chair. "Hell, greed, Billy. Pure and simple greed. They didn't want to share that water with anybody. If it had been found on government land, U.S. public land, then it would have belonged to everybody. The Castles wanted it for their cattle, their livestock."

Billy Vail studied the report a moment more before pitching it back on his desk. "You don't reckon the rest of the Castles were involved with the murder of those soldiers at the fort?"

Longarm shook his head. "No, I think that it was the damnedest unlucky coincidence that could have happened. I think that simpleminded Virgil, who halfway thought he was an Indian, had heard his daddy talking about the soldiers—and, of course, I'll never know the truth in this—and he either worked it out in his own head or had some help from Clell Martin, and decided that the soldiers were the enemy and that the way to eliminate them was to kill them. He had access to all those rifles, and I've got it out of the rest of the family that he was indeed a very good shot."

"You feel all right about letting Old Man Castle and those two boys go? I mean, you did have those charges filed against them for illegal cattle importation."

Longarm smiled slightly. "Well, I was kind of on thin ice about that."

Billy Vail gave a whoop. "Thin ice? Boy, that's an understatement. Thin ice? Hell, it was ninety-five degrees.

176

There wasn't no ice at all. What do you mean firing off a telegram to a fellow officer, getting him to get a bench warrant from a federal judge sent down to San Angelo? Hell, you could have gotten all our asses in a crack. What were you thinking about?"

Longarm said, "I was thinking about five dead soldiers, six after a while. That's what I was thinking about. I was thinking about how to unravel a knot when I couldn't find a way. The only thing that I could think of to do was to put some pressure on the Castles and see what came out of the jar. That's all I could figure out, Billy. I know, I probably exceeded my authority. . . ."

"Exceeded your authority? Boy, you sure have a quaint way of putting things, Mr. Custis Long."

Longarm sighed ruefully. It had taken a couple of days to clean the mess up. In the end, he had let Vernon Castle and his two sons go. They had gone willingly and they had certainly not been grateful. Even though Virgil had been simpleminded, he had been well loved by his family. Longarm could tell that Vernon Castle felt the loss keenly. The sheriff had been no friend of his at the end either. In fact, he had let Longarm know in no uncertain terms that he deeply resented the federal lawman and wished for any excuse to jail or to shoot him.

Only Captain Montrose and the soldiers had seemed grateful.

Billy Vail asked, "*Was* there a spring under the fort?"

Longarm shook his head. "I'll be damned if I know, Billy. They hadn't started digging by the time I left and I really don't care. All I know is that I wanted the hell out of San Angelo, Texas."

Billy Vail leaned back in his chair and cocked his head to one side. "Am I to understand that you found no diversion down there whatsoever? No female companionship to make the long hours and days pass faster?"

Longarm said nonchalantly, "Wherever would you have gotten an idea like that, Marshal Vail? I was on the job twenty-four hours a day. You sent me down there to do a job and that's all I did."

"Bullshit."

Longarm stood up. "I can't add a thing to it. The best I can figure, Clell Martin thought that it was still Reconstruction, and one day he took it into his head, either him or that simpleminded kid. They teamed up and decided to start killing soldiers. Clell convinced Virgil that he was an Indian and that his name was Running Wolf, or it might have been vice versa, it's hard to tell about crazy people. They both truly believed in what they were doing."

"How's your arm?"

Longarm shrugged. "It will work fine for whatever light duty I am going to get around here for a while."

Billy Vail gave him a big grin. He said, "Well . . . we'll just have to see what comes up."

Longarm pointed a finger at him. "Billy, you better not be sending me off any time soon. I've got business to do around here. I just put in two of the hardest weeks of my life, and I've got some easy time coming and I've got plans to make good use of it."

Billy Vail cackled. "By the way, the widow Shirley Dunn has come around a few times asking about you."

Longarm brightened. "She has?"

"Yeah, she has. But I'm gonna give you a piece of advice, Mr. Fast and Loose. That lady ain't gonna give you no milk unless you buy the cow. If I ever saw a marrying woman, that is one."

Longarm walked over to the door, took his hat off, and carefully brushed the brim before he set it back on his head.

He said in an offhanded voice, "Billy, have you ever spent a few nights in a whorehouse having drinks and dinner and, well . . . let's just call it dessert, and it didn't cost you a dime?"

"No, and you haven't either."

Longarm nodded and put his hand on the doorknob. He said, "Billy, there are some things in Heaven and Hell that you don't know about yet."

"I know one thing. Sometimes the truth ain't in you. Now go on and get out of here. Ten minutes with you is long enough for anybody."

Longarm opened the door and started out, and then he paused. He looked back at his boss and said, "Billy, I didn't like this one. I didn't like it at all. I had an old man who thought he was still fighting the Civil War. I had a simpleminded kid who thought he was a Comanche Indian fighting the long knives. And I had to kill them both. The wrong people got killed, Billy."

His boss said, "Are you telling me that you think that Old Man Castle and his sons knew?"

Longarm nodded. "I finally got it out of Glenn that they had found some spent cartridges from one of the Sharps rifles and that they had found some dust and dirt on one of them in the rack where they would normally be kept cleaned. They knew, all right."

Billy Vail said, "Then why didn't you hold them as accessories?"

Longarm shook his head. "Billy, it wouldn't have done any good. It would have been local jurisdiction and they would have never convicted a Castle. Not in that county.

Not in San Angelo. Besides, I figure that the townspeople and the Castles all deserve each other anyway."

Billy Vail said, "Probably you're right. Go on and get a drink and forget about it. You might have to forget about the widow Shirley Dunn too." He cackled.

Longarm said, "We'll see about that." He shut the door behind him and walked off through the outer office toward the hall, his mind finally turning to other things.

Only one thing kept bothering him, and would not go away no matter how hard he tried to look forward to the challenge of the Widow Dunn. He had finally succeeded in locating the missing horses of the dead soldiers. Other than the one Todd had run across and taken home, Longarm had found the five others on Vernon Castle's range. Now that in itself wasn't unexpected considering how much land Vernon Castle owned. But that didn't explain who had unsaddled and taken the bridles off the horses and penned them in a small corral at the very southern edge of the Castle property. It also didn't explain who had brought feed to the animals and who had decorated the horses with paint and feathers in the Comanche custom. Maybe Vernon Castle hadn't seen the horses himself, and maybe neither of his other sons had run across the little horse trap, but he was damned if he'd believe that such a strange circumstance had escaped all of Castle's line riders and that Castle hadn't been told about it.

Yes, he was convinced that Vernon Castle had known all along, had maybe known since the first soldier had been killed. And had done nothing about it, had not even taken steps to prevent it from happening again by privately locking his crazy son away somehow. But Longarm had not pursued the matter. It would have been impossible to prove. The last words he'd said to Vernon Castle had been: "Mister Castle, you are just as guilty of murder as Virgil. Maybe more so. And one of these days I'm going to have the pleasure of proving that. But for the time being you can just spend your time, until that time, walking as thin a line as you can. And you better keep looking over your shoulder, because you never know when I might be back here coming hard."

It had been all he could do. It had left him unsatisfied, but there had been no help for it. The evidence was too flimsy.

But that was past, and he stepped out into the Denver sunshine with a determination to doing something about another unsatisfied feeling he had—one that had been caused by Mrs. Shirley Dunn.

Watch for

LONGARM AND THE JERKWATER BUSTOUT

194th in the bold LONGARM series
from Jove

Coming in February!

If you enjoyed this book, subscribe now and get...

TWO FREE

A $7.00 VALUE—

If you would like to read more of the very best, most exciting, adventurous, action-packed Westerns being published today, you'll want to subscribe to True Value's Western Home Subscription Service.

Each month the editors of True Value will select the 6 very best Westerns from America's leading publishers for special readers like you. You'll be able to preview these new titles as soon as they are published, *FREE* for ten days with no obligation!

TWO FREE BOOKS

When you subscribe, we'll send you your first month's shipment of the newest and best 6 Westerns for you to preview. With your first shipment, two of these books will be yours as our introductory gift to you absolutely *FREE* (a $7.00 value), regardless of what you decide to do. If

you like them, as much as we think you will, keep all six books but pay for just 4 at the low subscriber rate of just $2.75 each. If you decide to return them, keep 2 of the titles as our gift. No obligation.

Special Subscriber Savings

When you become a True Value subscriber you'll save money several ways. First, all regular monthly selections will be billed at the low subscriber price of just $2.75 each. That's at least a savings of $4.50 each month below the publishers price. Second, there is never any shipping, handling or other hidden charges—*Free home delivery*. What's more there is no minimum number of books you must buy, you may return any selection for full credit and you can cancel your subscription at any time. A TRUE VALUE!